July 18, 2010

To Dale –

Very nice to meet you. Thanks for reading my book!

George Bird

BALLANTINE BOOKS NEW YORK

Letter to My Daughter

Letter to My Daughter

A NOVEL

GEORGE BISHOP

Published in the United States by Ballantine Books, an imprint of The Random House Publishing Group, a division of Random House, Inc., New York.

BALLANTINE and colophon are registered trademarks of Random House, Inc.

Grateful acknowledgment is made to Hal Leonard Corporation for permission to reprint excerpts from *Just My Imagination (Running Away with Me)*. Words and music by Norman J. Whitfield and Barrett Strong, copyright © 1970 (renewed 1998) Jobete Music Co., Inc. All rights controlled and administered by EMI Blackwood Music Inc. on behalf of Stone Agate Music (A Division of Jobete Music Co., Inc.). All Rights Reserved. International Copyright Secured Used by Permission

ISBN-13: 978-0-345-51598-8

Printed in the United States of America

Book design by Mary A. Wirth

FOR MY FATHER

I shall but love thee better after death.

—ELIZABETH BARRETT BROWNING,
Sonnets from the Portuguese, NO. 43

Letter to My Daughter

I

MARCH 22, 2004

. . .

BATON ROUGE

Dear Elizabeth,

How to begin this? It's early morning and I'm sitting here wondering where you are, hoping you're all right. I haven't slept since you left. Your father says there's no sense in phoning the police yet; you're probably just blowing off steam, and you'll be back as soon as you run out of money or the car runs out of gas, whichever comes first. I shouldn't be so hard on myself, he says. What with the way you spoke to me last night, it would take more forbearance than anyone's capable of not to react the way I did, and besides, it wasn't even that much of a slap.

Still, I blame myself. I keep seeing the look on your face as you brought your hand up to your cheek—the shock, the hurt, then the cold stare that bordered on hatred. When I heard the back door close in the middle of the night, I thought to myself, *Well. There she goes*. But it was only when I was standing on the driveway in my nightgown watching the taillights of my car disappear down the street that I understood just how bad this has become.

I'll try not to insult you by saying I know how it feels to be fifteen. (I can see you rolling your eyes.) But believe it or not, I was your age once, and I had the same ugly fights with my parents. And I promised myself that if I ever had a daughter, I would be a better parent to her than mine were to me. My daughter, I told myself, would never have to endure the same inept upbringing that I did. I would be the perfect mother: patient and understanding, kind and sensible. I would listen to all my girl's problems, help her when she needed it, and together we would build a bridge of trust that would carry us both into old age. Our relationship—it seemed so simple then—would be marked by love, not war.

Well. Things don't always turn out the way we want them to, do they? Sometimes when I'm yelling at you for coming in late, or criticizing your choice of friends, or your taste in clothing, or your apparent indifference to anything having to do with family or school or future, I hear my mother's voice coming out of my mouth. My mother's very words, even. In spite of all my best intentions, I find myself becoming her. And you, of course, become me, reacting the same way I reacted when I was your age, revisiting all the same hurts that I suffered, and so completing one great big vicious circle of ineptitude.

I want to stop this. I've thought and thought, and I'm not sure how to go about it, except maybe to make it a rule to do everything that my mother didn't do and not to do everything that she did—a crude way to right the wrongs, no doubt, and not altogether fair to my mother, who on occasion could be a decent person.

But one thing I've realized that my mother never did—and this was perhaps her greatest failing as a parent—the one thing she never did was to give me any good honest advice about growing up. Oh, she gave me plenty of rules, to be sure. She was a fountain of rules: sit up straight, keep your legs together, don't run, don't shout, don't frown, don't wear too much makeup or boys will think you're a tramp. But she never told me what I really wanted to know: How does a girl grow up? How does a girl make it through that miserable age called adolescence and finally get to become a woman?

This was something I thought I might be able to help you with. I always pictured us sitting down together and having a talk, mother to daughter. You'd take your earphones out, I'd turn off the TV. Your father would be out running errands and so we'd have the whole afternoon to ourselves. In this talk, I would begin by telling you, as straightforwardly as I could, the story of my own adolescence. My intention would be not to shock or embarrass you, but to try and show you we're not all that different, you and I. I do know what it's like to be your age: I was there once, after all. I lived through it. And hearing the mistakes I made, you might learn from them and not have to repeat them. You could be spared my scars, in other words, so that the life you grow up in might be better than the one I had. Today, I thought, would be a good time for us to have this talk, your fifteenth birthday.

As nice as it sounds, that probably isn't going to happen, is it? I think I made sure of that last night when I slapped you and drove you from our home. I could hardly blame you now if you don't want to listen to me. It'll take more than apologies for you to begin to trust me again.

So what I've decided to do is that while I'm sitting here waiting for you to return, I'll write down in a letter everything I've always meant to tell you but never have. Maybe a letter is a poor substitute for the talk I always wanted us to have. But it's a start at least, and I hope you'll find it in yourself, if not today then sometime in the future, to accept it in the same spirit that I write it. Think of it as my birthday present to you—something that my mother never told me, but that I'll endeavor now with all my heart to tell you: the truth about how a girl grows up. The truth about life.

I'm on my third cup of coffee now and there's still no sign of you. Your dad's out back mowing the grass like nothing ever happened. I'm not going to get all panicky, not yet. It's still early, and I intend to keep my mind from imagining the worst. But I do hope you'll be back in time to spend at least some of your birthday with us. I do hope you're okay, Liz.

II

"Begin at the beginning," Sister Mary Margaret always told us.

The beginning of this, I suppose, is 1969, when I was your age, a freshman in high school. We still had the farm then—you know, the old house in Zachary where your Mams and Gramps used to live. Zachary wasn't like it is today. It really was the sticks then. I often felt we might've been living on Mars for all the contact we had with the rest of the world. Our house was at the end of a gravel road, a mile and a half from any other home, and I mostly hated living there. I was only a farm girl in the sense that I could ride a horse and, if forced to, I could milk a cow. But as a teenager, generally I wanted nothing to do with cows and horses and alfalfa crops. I went to school, read magazines, and watched *The Partridge Family* on TV on Friday nights, suspecting that everyone in the world lived a more glamorous and exciting life than I did. Probably a lot like you.

Your grandparents were Baptists, as you know, and certainly more strict with me than I've ever been with you. They were what, if you were feeling generous, you might call conservative. If you were feeling more honest, you might call them narrow-minded and racist. Mom loathed *The Partridge Family*—thought it was a disgrace that a single mother would tramp around the country with all those long-haired kids in a painted school bus. And Dad—well, your grandfather loathed the blacks. Sorry to say.

The schools in Louisiana were just then getting integrated, if you can believe that. I'm sure I've told you this before. Nineteen seventy was the year all the white students from Zachary High and all the black students from Lincoln High were to be mixed up together at one school. You can imagine the commotion this announcement caused, especially among people like your grandfather. There were rallies, the National Guard was called in, the KKK was called in . . .

And my parents began talking of sending me away to Catholic boarding school in Baton Rouge. Better that, my father said, than letting me spend one single day sitting side by side in a classroom with those "god damn coloreds."

Now here's the part I never told you about, at least not in any detail. You've only known him as "a boy I grew up with," but he had a name. It was Tim Prejean.

Tim was seventeen, a senior at Zachary High School when I was a freshman. We met—or I should say, we first spoke—at the Freshman-Senior Get Acquainted Dance. I was standing with my girlfriends near the bleachers in the gym, all of us in our pressed bell-bottoms and platform shoes, when he came over and asked me to dance. "Hey, um, Laura," he said, or something to that effect. "Wanna dance?"

I was surprised he knew my name. We rode the same bus

to school in the morning, and I'd seen him in the cafeteria, but we had never before openly acknowledged one another. Tim wasn't one of the more popular boys at school. His shoulders were too narrow and his neck too thin, and he went in for the geek clubs like the Eagle Scouts and Ham Radio Enthusiasts. But he had wonderful dark brown hair that hung down low over his forehead so that it almost covered his right eye, and on the night of the Freshman-Senior Get Acquainted Dance he wore aftershave and a blue blazer over a dashing white turtleneck. The song, I remember, was "Sugar, Sugar" by the Archies—a dumb song, and not an easy one to dance to. Still, he was a senior, and I was a freshman, and there were crepe paper streamers and colored lights overhead—probably someone had spiked the punch, too—and taken all together, it was enough to make our meeting that night, no matter how clumsy, feel thrilling and romantic.

We began dating, although we didn't call it that. We sat together on the bus going to school. We sat together at lunch. We sat together on the bus coming home, and then we talked to each other on the phone in the evening. When we could, we met at the Greenwoods Mall on the weekends. It was always a little awkward because he had his friends and I had mine, and there was the two-year age difference between us. But the biggest problem was his family.

The Prejeans weren't "landowners," as I had been taught to call our own family. The Prejeans came from Cajun stock, and anyone who spoke any French in Zachary in those days was considered little better than black. "Swamp rats" my father called them, or worse, when he was joking with his farm buddies, "bayou niggers."

Tim's father, Jack Prejean, owned a dusty radio and TV

repair shop in downtown Zachary that hardly anyone visited anymore—anyone in this case meaning white folks like us. His shop was on a mixed street, as it was called, and most of his customers were black. If that wasn't bad enough, the Prejeans lived in a camping trailer parked in a clump of woods at the far edge of Zachary, out past where Kleinpeter Dairy used to be. By most outward appearances, in other words, Tim's family lived up to the stereotypes people like my father had of people like the Prejeans.

But the Prejeans, I knew, hadn't always been this poor. They had once lived in a tidy two-bedroom house within walking distance of the elementary school. Mr. Prejean's radio and TV repair shop had once done a respectable business, too, before Greenwoods Mall was built and people started vacating the downtown. But it was Mrs. Prejean's disease that finally and truly ruined the family.

This was before Tim and I began going out together, and I only knew the Prejeans insomuch as everyone knew everyone else in Zachary in those days. But even I knew about the disease. That was how people whispered about it: "the disease." It was, I'd heard rumored, syphilis, and what little I knew of that made it sound especially ugly and obscene, something dimly associated with soldiers and black people and Frenchmen. Mrs. Prejean—Suzy—made occasional outings into town during the early stages of her illness, and a Suzy Prejean sighting was always the subject of gruesome telephone gossip among our neighborhood moms. The school bus passed the Prejeans's house every day coming and going, and I would sit pressed by the window watching for her ghostly figure hiding behind the white curtains, wondering what the disease looked like, imagining the house itself to be pale and radiant with sickness.

Jack Prejean didn't have any medical insurance, and a year of hospital bills took all his money and most of what he owned. When his poor wife finally died, in a wild display of grief and love he sold their house to pay for her funeral. It was a huge affair, with an extravagant velvet-lined brass casket laid out on the altar among an astonishing array of flowers and candles. There was a full choir, with an organist brought in from Baton Rouge, and a whole gang of priests and servers in red and white robes swinging censers. After the service we followed a sleek black hearse and three rented limousines to the cemetery, where we watched as the beautiful coffin was lowered into the ground below an elaborate white marble memorial of a life-sized woman in classical dress reaching out to pluck a rose from a vine. The Suzy Prejean funeral was such a big event in Zachary that year, in fact, that people who barely knew the Prejeans, people who didn't really give a good damn about them—people like my mother—turned up in their best Jacqueline Kennedy outfits at St. Aloysius Catholic Church to be a part of it. Funerals were especially popular in those days.

The extravagant service, though, still wasn't enough to redeem the character of Jack's wife in the eyes of the town, or at least in the eyes of my parents. Even when we found out it wasn't syphilis but ovarian cancer that had killed Suzy Prejean, my parents still figured, in their own mean way, that the Prejeans had got what they deserved.

"All the flowers in the world can't buy salvation," was how my mother put it.

Two years later when Tim and I began seeing each other, a vague cloud of disgrace still hung over his family name. Tim himself seemed quietly ashamed of his mother's death, and his father's poor downtown shop, and their camping trailer out in the woods. So when he invited me to come visit, it was as if he was offering to reveal to me a secret part of himself, like a wound on his person, and I felt privileged and trusted.

Tim borrowed his father's service truck to take me to their place late one Saturday afternoon. "It's not much," he warned me as we drove out Highway 19 toward Slaughter. "I hope you won't mind." We turned off the pavement past Kleinpeter Dairy onto a red clay road where a few small houses stood scattered here and there among the trees. You know the kind of place: dirt roads, dirt yards, dirt gardens. Frustration and anger and sadness turned inward to become poverty.

Mr. Prejean—Jack, he told me to call him—was desperately hospitable. Shaking my hand, he said how much he'd heard about me and how pleased he was to meet me. Like his son, Jack was thin, almost scrawny. He had on a neat gray repairman's uniform and black-rimmed eyeglasses, and wore his black hair slicked over to one side. Jack had set up a metal camp table for us under the pines, where he served me and Tim RC Cola and mixed nuts in plastic bowls with paper party napkins. He kept apologizing for the lack of amenities. I think I was the first houseguest they'd ever had.

What did we talk about? It couldn't have been much; I was only fifteen, Tim only seventeen, and Jack an unpracticed host. We talked about homework, I remember. Jack was up late nights himself these days, he said, studying to become an insurance sales agent, so he knew what it was like for us kids. He kept offering me more RC Colas, and I kept accepting just to be polite, until I had to go to the bathroom. Jack pointed me to the toilet in the trailer. I couldn't miss it, he joked—just go through the entrance hall, past the master bedroom, and I'd find it opposite the kitchen. Shout if I got lost.

The tiny size of the trailer and the sight of the few belongings the men shared (Old Spice, Brylcreem, *Popular Electronics*) made the space feel unbearably intimate. Coming out of the toilet cabinet I paused, trying to imagine what it must have been like for them to live there. An empty aluminum pot sat on a two-burner hot plate; beside it on the counter were three unopened cans of Campbell's chicken noodle soup—dinner, I supposed. At one end of the trailer was a built-in bed; three steps away at the other end of the trailer was a fold-down table covered with Tim's schoolbooks and Mr. Prejean's study guides from State Farm Insurance. The only decoration in the whole trailer was a framed color photograph on the wall above the table. I bent in for a closer look.

It must've been taken before her sickness. Suzy Prejean was leaning back on a swing, her long black hair hanging down, her bare tanned legs kicked straight out from beneath a polka-dotted dress. Her eyes were squeezed shut, her bright red lips opened wide as she laughed up at the blue sky. A smaller, younger Tim in a cowboy outfit pushed her from behind. The shadow of the photographer, who could only have been Jack himself, slanted across the ground to the right, completing the family triad. Knowing the way things turned out only made the scene that much more heart wrenching.

Tim stepped up into the trailer to find me looking at the photo. He stopped behind me and rested his hands on my shoulders.

"Your mom—she's gorgeous," I told him. This simple undeniable fact cast the Prejeans in a whole new light for me, making Tim and his father appear at once more admirable and tragic in my eyes. "I had no idea she was so pretty."

"Even more than that," he whispered over my shoulder.

I leaned back into his chest. And if you were to ask when I first knew I loved Tim, I would have to say it was then.

. . .

Up until that time, I had kept Tim a secret from my parents. But after he invited me to his home, I felt obliged to invite him to mine. The truth is I wasn't worried so much about Tim as I was about my father. Compared to gentle Mr. Prejean, my father seemed like a brute, and I was afraid of what he might do or say when I brought Tim home. But we had reached that stage in the relationship when you need to meet one another's families—not just for the sake of getting their approval, but because you feel proud of what you have and want them to see it.

The evening went badly. My mother was uncomfortable having Tim in her parlor. It was, I knew, on account of Mrs. Prejean's disease, and of Mr. Prejean living with his son in a trailer in the woods, which taken together made them worse even than the Partridge Family. Serving Tim macaroons, sitting and speaking with him from the sofa opposite, my mother assumed that same stiff-faced expression she got whenever she had to perform some unpleasant chore, like gutting a chicken or throwing slops to the pigs. My father, for his part, wasted no time in getting to the issue of Mr. Prejean's repair shop, and wasn't it a shame what the coloreds had done to ruin the downtown, and frankly he didn't see how Jack could tolerate doing business with those people, and what did Tim have to say about that?

It was a test, I knew. In my father's eyes, Tim was barely one rung above black himself, and the only way for him to prove himself to be good and truly white would be to join my father in belittling the Negroes. Tim, though, to his everlasting credit, made the honorable choice of defending his father's customers, saying that without their patronage the shop would've closed a long time ago, and anyway, from an electronics point of view, a TV was a TV no matter who owned it. Then he went on to declare that some of their closest neighbors were black people, and they'd never had any problem with them at all, in fact found them to be quite friendly and decent, probably the best neighbors they'd ever had. This led, as I knew it inevitably would, to the topic of the integration of the public schools, and my father's claim that he was "no racist," but to be rational about the matter, mixing would have no benefit for anybody. No one wanted it—not the blacks, not the whites—and to insist on it was worse than undemocratic, it was criminal. Tim tried to reason with him, but he had the disadvantage of being younger and more polite and smarter than my father. He finally lost his patience, though, when my father brought out his favorite argument, throwing it down like a trump card on the table: the secret scientific study done at Louisiana State University that proved the inferior intelligence of the Negroid races. They had the skull measurements! Brains in formaldehyde! Right there in the basement at LSU! Those were the scientific facts. What about that, Tim? Huh?

"I can't believe this. I can't believe I'm having this conversation," Tim said, standing to leave. "I'm sorry, Mr. Jenkins, sir, but you . . . you're just plain ignorant."

Well. My father rose, his hands coming up in fists like he was ready for a fight. No swamp rat was going to call him ignorant. I jumped up to try and defend Tim, and as he and my father traded words, my mother, her face by now so hard that it looked like it would crack into a hundred pieces, could only sputter uselessly from her perch on the sofa, "Now now! Now now!"

Later, sitting beside Tim outside in his father's service truck, I felt so ashamed that I wanted to disappear into the seat. Why had God given me two such horrible parents? How could they be so mean and awful? What had I ever done to deserve them?

"You're not them, Laura. You're not them," Tim whispered as he wiped the tears from my face with his fingertips.

"Never be afraid of the truth, girls."

That was another saying of Sister Mary Margaret's, and one of my favorites. This next part of the story is important, though it's difficult to tell. Still, I'm sure you know more about sex than I ever did when I was your age, so I don't suppose anything I write will shock you. I'm just giving you notice, is all.

It was the Christmas holidays and my parents had gone out to visit friends for the evening. You can picture winter in Zachary—you've been there enough yourself when you were younger. In that flat delta landscape of pine trees and sugarcane fields, winter comes as a relief from the heat and terrible humidity suffered throughout the rest of the year. It was my favorite season, and the only time I felt any real affection for the farm. The air became crisp and clear, the pond froze over at the edges, squadrons of brown pelicans flew overhead. Making pumpkin pie with my mother in the kitchen, or carrying in firewood with my father, I could imagine myself becoming reconciled with my parents and creating a life with them on the farm. I could imagine a future where parents and child were friends instead of combatants, allies in a peaceful, sensible world.

Tim came over later that night, after my parents had left, to pick me up for a movie date at the mall. Although my parents hadn't explicitly forbidden me to see him, it was plain they didn't approve, and so Tim took pains to avoid meeting them, and I took pains not to mention his name around the house. They didn't know I was still seeing him, in other words.

Tim stoked the fire in the parlor while I went to get ready. I remember chatting to him from my bedroom off the hall as I dressed, him answering me from time to time through the open doorway. When I came back into the front room he was still squatting down in front of the fireplace, adjusting the logs with a poker—

Have you ever seen a man do that? I'm sure you have: the way they poke at burning logs with a kind of natural assurance—turning them over, prying them up on one end, settling them down again—as if tending a fire was something they were born for, something inherited in the genes, generation after generation, going all the way back to people living in cabins and caves. Tim was talking out of the corner of his mouth, his chin turned slightly from the fire, thinking I was still in the bedroom. I held back in the doorway to watch him.

Like I've said, Tim wasn't a big boy, but he had on his red plaid barn coat that evening with a nice pair of jeans and a gray muffler looped around his neck. The side of his face caught the glow from the fire. Watching him in secret while he went on talking and poking at the logs, so at ease, so content, I felt I was seeing him at his most private. This, I thought, was exactly what Tim was like when he was most alone. And it was a most admirable and inspiring sight.

I'm only trying to put this like I remember it. Outside was cold, inside was warm. The fire was burning. We were alone and my parents weren't due back for another couple of hours. We did just what any fifteen-year-old girl and seventeen-year-old boy would do in that situation.

I turned off the light by the door and hugged Tim from behind. He squirmed, chuckling, as I kissed his neck and ear. He turned around and lay me down on the rug. Then he hovered above me, gently stroking my hair as he studied my face. His eyes ticked back and forth, like he was divining signs of our future together in my features. He looked so serious that it began to make me uncomfortable.

"Why'd you ever ask me to dance?" I asked him finally.

"What?"

"That night at the Freshman-Senior Dance. Why'd you pick me?"

He thought about this for a moment.

"After my mom died, it was like everyone was afraid to talk to me. Like I was contagious or something. I remember you used to look at me so pitifully—like you were the only one who knew how hard it was.

"One morning—you probably don't even remember

this—one morning you smiled at me. I was coming on the bus and you were sitting in the back, watching me. You made this crooked kind of half-smile, like you were trying to cheer me up. It lasted maybe only half a second. You probably don't even remember it. But it made me feel a whole lot better that day."

I did remember.

"And so that's why I asked you to dance that night. I just never—" He stopped.

"What?"

He hesitated, moving his lips like he was working up to say something.

I prodded him with my knee. "Say it."

"I just never . . . I never in my life thought I could get so lucky."

At a time like this it's not the words so much as the sentiment. This one came deep and true from inside him, and he was offering it to me, handing it to me, like something unspeakably fragile and precious. And him trusting me like that opened up something inside of me.

Understand that before that night Tim and I had done little more than kiss. They were good kisses, to be sure. But I'd been brought up Baptist, and things learned in Bible school, no matter how absurd, have a way of sticking with you. And Tim, of course, was too polite to ever push himself on me. But that night everything was just so perfect that there wasn't any question of right or wrong, good or bad.

I helped him take off his barn jacket, his sweater, and his blue jeans. Tim was shy about his body, so I had never even seen him without a T-shirt before. His build was still that of a teenager's—a little bony, slender, and perfectly smooth. As he helped me off with my clothes, he grew in confidence, until eventually we were divested of all shame and lay marveling at one another's features. That evening before the fire, transformed by trust and love, we were both as young and beautiful and flawless as God had intended.

Probably I shouldn't be telling you this. But people can say whatever they want about what we did next. They can call it whatever they like, they can sell it and profane it however they want: I know that what we did was a good thing. And I know that no matter what anyone says, teenagers are fully capable of loving one another. At a certain age, teenagers may even be the most capable: before their minds are poisoned by hurt and doubt, before the world steps in with its age-old hates and prejudices to destroy whatever childhood notions of love still linger in their hearts.

I won't embarrass you with the details—you know well enough what I'm talking about. Let me just say that, together on the rug that night, we discovered a sympathy for one another that bordered on the divine. Call it our marriage. What was mine became his, and what was his was mine. Where had we learned to do all that? From no one. From our own God-given instincts. At the end, I remember, I cried a little. Tim whispered promises until I felt reassured. Sighing, laughing, wrapped up in each other's arms, we didn't see the headlights sweeping the walls of the parlor or hear the footsteps crossing the front porch before my parents stepped into the room and found us.

The scene that followed was so ugly that even now I remember it as a hellish red blur. My mother screamed and covered her mouth. My father let out a string of obscenities. I scrabbled to hide myself behind the sofa while my father hauled Tim up from the floor and began beating him. Gripping his skinny arm in one hand, he slammed punch after punch at his head. "Hold her back!" he ordered my mother when I tried to stop him. She caught me by the arm and swung me around. An end table was overturned, a lamp was broken. We became like monsters, wailing and thrashing about the firelit den as our shadows danced like demons on the walls until at last my father, swearing in the vilest language, kicked Tim, bleeding and naked, down the front porch steps while I stood back in the hallway with a rug wrapped around myself, screaming, "I hate you! I hate you! I hate you!"

I was locked into my bedroom and banned forever from seeing "that degenerate" again. And the very next week, before the end of Christmas vacation, my parents brought me down to Baton Rouge for an admissions interview at Sacred Heart Academy.

III

Well. It's past noon and you're still not home.

During a break from writing I went up and checked your room. I didn't go through your private things, don't worry, but I see you took your daypack and toothbrush. I phoned Missy DeSalle's house, but no one was home except the maid and she didn't know anything. So then I phoned around to all your other friends—all the friends I know of, at least—but they say they haven't heard from you.

I wouldn't be surprised if you went with Missy to Fort Lauderdale after all. That's what this is all about it, isn't it? That's how our fight began, as I remember: our refusal to let you go to Florida for spring break, and then the arguing and the shouting and the cursing. Call me a hypocrite, call me any ugly names you want, I still don't see how we're being unreasonable. You're fifteen years old, for god's sake. What kind of parents would we be if we let you spend a week in Florida, unchaperoned, with a bunch of stoned high school seniors?

After your father came in for lunch I finally convinced him to phone the police. He didn't want to. He says you'll be in a world of trouble if they find you driving with just a learner's permit and we ought to try and avoid that for now, if only for your sake. I said we ought to be more worried about your safety than about your driving record, and if you broke the law, well, you broke the law and there was nothing we could do about that now.

The police, as it turns out, weren't very helpful. They said they don't take reports of a missing person unless it's been at least twenty-four hours, and then only if the disappearance is of a suspicious nature. I said it was, your father disagreed. Then they gave us the number for the Department of Juvenile Services. In case we needed help with ungovernable children, they said, we should contact them for an interview and a probation officer would be assigned to our case. I took the phone and said you weren't ungovernable, just missing, and what good were the police if they couldn't help people, wasn't that what they were hired to do, to serve and protect and whatever? And so on like this until the woman on the other end of the line lost patience and hung up. After that I phoned all the hospitals in the parish. No one matching your description, thank god.

So just now I've sent your father out to look for you in the car. He says it's a ridiculous idea: If you're already in Florida, what's the point? And if you're not in Florida, how's he going to find you in a city of half a million people? He says he'll go to Home Depot first to buy some fertilizer for the lawn and then he'll go check the shopping mall. He says you're probably there trying on clothes. I said he shouldn't be making jokes at a time like this.

If it's your intention to punish us for being too mean, or too strict, or too whatever, well then, you've succeeded. We get the message. We'll sit down, we'll talk this out and find some compromise. You can come home now. We won't be mad, I promise. We just need to know you're safe. You hear so many terrible stories on the news these days. I turned on the TV for the noon news, hoping somehow I might see something about you—crazy, I know. What I saw instead was another report about that twelve-year-old girl in Prairieville who went missing last year. They found her, locked in a soundproofed basement below the home of a local couple. A middle-aged man and woman, no doubt with friends and jobs and club memberships, they could've been anyone you passed on the sidewalk. But the things they did to her—you can't imagine human beings capable of such depravity. Horrible things, things you don't even want to think about. God help that poor girl.

Okay. Now you see why I get so worried. Pardon the interruption. I've set my mind to tell you this story, so I'll get back to it now.

IV

"Oxymoron."

Do you know what that means? Sister Mary Margaret taught it to us. It's when you put two contradictory words or ideas together for literary effect, as in "cruel kindness" or "sweet pain." One phrase that I always considered to be an especially good example of an oxymoron, and one that was popular back in 1970, is "free love."

Could there be two more contradictory words? When has love ever been free? When did it ever come without a cost?

When my parents drove me down to Baton Rouge for the interview at Sacred Heart Academy, I was sick at heart with hurt and loss. I'd spent most of the weekend crying in bed, not eating meals and refusing to speak to my parents. My mother wept outside my door and wondered where they had gone wrong. My father slammed around the house cursing the blacks and perverts and hippie Jews who had destroyed the morals and decency in the country. If the integration of Zachary public schools had first made them think of sending me away to a private boarding school, then catching me on the floor of the living room with Tim Prejean convinced them that this was the only smart thing to do. They only wanted what was best for me, after all. Locked in my bedroom, hearing them talk this through, I became halfway convinced myself that what they said was true, and that what Tim and I had done was indeed sinful, and that the best recourse for everyone was separation.

I sat in the back of the car, looking out the side window at the bare trees and winter fields blurring past. My parents sat up front, exchanging barely a dozen words between them during the one-hour drive to Baton Rouge. The air from the heater was warm and stale, heavy with our compounded shame, anger, and guilt.

In the principal's office at Sacred Heart we all sat in a semicircle in front of Sister Evelyn's desk. You can imagine the scene: a cross on the wall, a framed portrait of the pope, a painting of Jesus pointing at his glowing heart. My father leaned forward with his hands on the knees of his trousers, trying to appear gentlemanly and sincere. My mother sat upright with her ankles crossed primly below her chair, wearing old-fashioned black shoes and an ugly furry gray wool dress with oversized buttons, an outfit that she somehow thought looked Catholic.

You remember how much your grandfather distrusted the Catholics. To him, Catholics were almost as bad as Jews. But in the interview with Sister Evelyn, I saw my father's eyes take on that same crafty, guilty look he got whenever he was bargaining with the manager of the feed store or wrangling for handouts from the Farm Bureau. He spoke about how they had always wanted to provide me, their only daughter, with a good moral education, and what an excellent reputation Sacred Heart Academy had, not only in the field of morality but also in the field of academics, and how although we were not ourselves of the Catholic persuasion, we nevertheless had always held a great respect for priests and nuns and people like that, and anyway we were all Christians under the skin, weren't we? My mother nodded and agreed with whatever he said, adding, outlandishly, that she always wished that she could have gone to a Catholic school herself. Lies, of course, all of them. But my parents couldn't very well come out and say the truth, which was, "We're here because we hate the coloreds and we caught our daughter having sex on the living room floor with a trailer boy."

After they had finished speaking, Sister Evelyn turned to me. "And why do you want to come to Sacred Heart, Laura?"

I hadn't expected the question. It wasn't something my parents had expected, either. They watched me anxiously from their chairs, my father's jawbone flexing beneath the skin of his rough cheeks, my mother's face fixed into a crooked, tense smile. Sister Evelyn tilted her head to one side below the picture of Jesus.

At that point I had no feeling one way or another about Sacred Heart. But I despised my parents just then, for all they'd done and for all they stood for—their bigotry, their hypocrisy, their low-down meanness. And I knew my relationship with Tim was as good as dead, so staying at home in Zachary or going away to Baton Rouge hardly made any difference to me. For the hopeless, one prison is as good as the next.

Sister Evelyn waited for my response. Behind her back, Jesus pointed to his burning red heart, commanding me to speak.

"I want a better life for myself," I said at last. Which was the truth at least as far as I could tell it.

I've sometimes wondered since then why the school took

me in. I suspect Sister Evelyn knew there was more to our story than what we were telling. We weren't the first non-Catholic family to come knocking for admission since the integration of the Louisiana public schools was announced, after all. And if that wasn't the reason, well then, everyone knew that Sacred Heart was where families sent problem girls who needed reform. None of this was spoken of openly, of course. And regardless of the truth of the situation, I believe the nuns in their own blinkered way preferred to see my enrollment simply as one more victory for the faith: a poor Baptist farm girl from Zachary had been brought into the fold. One more ransomed pagan baby, saved.

Sunday evening before the start of classes for the new year 1970, Sister Agatha led me and my parents down a black-and-white linoleum tiled corridor to my room. Sacred Heart Academy used to have one wing of the convent building reserved for a small number of boarding students. That year, I remember Sister Agatha telling us, there were thirty-two—"Now thirty-three, of course, counting you."

It seemed like all thirty-two came to their doors to witness my arrival. I had my suitcase, my mother carried the linens, my father had a cardboard box full of books and things. Sister Agatha explained to us about the house rules, the hall phone, my work-study obligations. My new roommate, Melissa Thayer from Hammond, watched as my mother hugged me goodbye, and my father, pushed forward by my mother, kissed me stiffly on the cheek. He gave me five dollars and they left.

"Welcome to the nunnery," Melissa said when they had all gone. She was tall and thin, with sharp features and an abrupt manner of speaking. "Laura Jenkins," she said, looking me up and down. "Did you just come from the farm, or what?"

"Zachary," I said.

"Oh. Wow. Sorry," Melissa said.

What has been the most lonesome night in your life so far? Could you pick out one, say, "That was the worst of them all"? For me it would have to be that first night at Sacred Heart. Separated from my boyfriend, abandoned by my parents, I felt like the most unloved fifteen-year-old girl in the universe. As the stark reality of my situation sank in, I was filled with a loneliness that ached in every bone and tissue of my body. My mother and father weren't going to be overcome with remorse and return the next day to bring me home. Tim wasn't going to appear on the lawn below the window to carry me off in his arms. Nothing was going to get better. Pale winter moonlight shone through the barred window at the head of the room, casting a gray grid on the floor. Buried down under a too-thin blanket, I tried to stifle my sobs so as not to disturb my new roommate. Sometime around midnight, Melissa called from across the room:

"Do you mind? I'm trying to sleep over here."

. . .

To be a high school transfer student is hard, but to be a midyear high school transfer student is even harder. Most of the girls at Sacred Heart came from old-time Baton Rouge families, daughters of daughters of alumnae, and so a new out-of-towner like me was a great curiosity. I might have been a chimpanzee just delivered from the zoo for all the stares I got that first morning. I kept tugging at my new uniform; it didn't seem to fit right—it was too tight in all the wrong places and too loose in the others. I was wearing ugly thick-soled lace-ups instead of the smart penny loafers the other girls wore, and I couldn't get my navy blue knee socks to stay up the way they were supposed to. In almost every class I had to stand, say my name, where I was from, and what I liked to do. "Tell the class something about yourself, Laura," the nuns asked. That last question stumped me until I hit on "I like to read"—which at least pleased the Freshman Rhetoric teacher, Sister Mary Margaret.

At lunch I ended up sitting at a table in the cafeteria with a bunch of other misfits. A more forlorn group of girls you couldn't find. There were the girls on hardship scholarships, like me; there was one pathologically shy Asian girl, Soo Chee Chong, who never spoke a word and was ashamed of her name; there was Christy Lee, one of five black students at the school, who crept around so silently that she looked like she wished she were invisible; and there was Anne Harding, locked in a monstrous steel neck brace that didn't allow her to turn her head independent of her body. We were, I later learned, what the other girls called the charity cases.

Have you ever wondered why so many unfortunate people seem so spiteful? Why they so often refuse—despise, even—efforts made to help them? I know why. Because I sat at their table, I know why. Within a week at Sacred Heart Academy, I had learned what every charity case knows: that any act of kindness can also be cruel. If some girl happened to be nice to us, we knew she was only being nice out of a sense of Christian duty, because she felt she *had* to be nice to us. And if some other girl wasn't nice, well, that only proved how rotten all people really were at the core. So we, the charity cases, were doomed to be doubly bitter: bitter when rejected, and bitter when not.

Lucky for you, Liz, you don't seem to have this problem. You've always had plenty of friends, and none of them charity cases as far as I can tell. Still, I suspect that all of us, no matter how fortunate, feel like charity cases at some time or another in our lives.

. . .

My only consolation that first week at Sacred Heart came in the form of a letter, delivered to me by Sister Agatha late one afternoon at the dormitory. Even now, thirty-four years later, I remember the shape and feel of that envelope, with the Zachary return address in the upper left corner, the six-cent Dwight D. Eisenhower stamp in the right, and my name square in the middle. And inside, the folded sheet of notebook paper covered with his handwriting; handwriting that was so like his character, teetering between an adolescent awkwardness and a touchingly earnest effort to appear upright and manly.

"Dear Laura," Tim began. He went on to say how he wasn't much of a writer, but he wanted me to know that he missed me more than I could imagine. If anyone was to blame for my being sent away, he wrote, it was him. He was the man, after all, and he should've been more responsible for our safety that evening. Not that he regretted it, though. That night, no matter what came after, would always stand for him as the best night of his life. Because it was that night, he wrote, that he found out what true love is.

Thus began our correspondence, one that would continue for as long as I was a student at Sacred Heart, and that, in the early days at least, was like a lifeline, tethering me to a tree of hope in an otherwise bleak landscape.

I wrote back right away to tell Tim how much I loved and missed him, too. I wrote about my first miserable night in the dormitory, and my roommate, Melissa, and the charity cases at the lunch table. I wrote him letters in the back of my notebook from the last row of Freshman Science while Sister Helen—Yellin' Helen—lectured on the periodic table. And in the afternoons, while other girls were out flirting with boys from Cathedral High School, or going to piano lessons, or attending basketball practice, I would write to Tim from the library, long shadows slanting across the dusty tabletops as I emptied out my loneliness onto page after page of white paper.

I came to rely desperately on his responses. My heart jumped up whenever Sister Hagatha-Agatha delivered another letter to me in the afternoon at the dormitory, frowning in poorly disguised disapproval behind her old-lady eyeglasses. Who ever knew so much happiness could be contained in one small envelope? If Tim missed more than a few days, I would become anxious and dash off two letters at once, wondering what was wrong. He would write back apologizing, saying how he'd been out hunting with his buddies over the weekend and so wasn't able to answer my last letter as soon as he would've liked, but not to worry, I was always on his mind. I'd write again: How could he even think about going out hunting with his friends and having fun when I was locked up here in this prison for girls? Didn't he have any feelings at all? And why had he signed "Love" instead of his usual "Love always" in the closing of his last letter? Maybe he didn't miss me as much as I missed him. Maybe what he called "the best night of my life" wasn't so great after all.

Maybe we'd be better off just forgetting that anything ever happened between us. . . . And so on, until he would send me a reassuring letter by Express Mail, filled to the margins with the most tender sentiments a girl could ever want to read. On paper, I learned, even arguments can be beautiful.

I suppose even at the time a part of me relished the melodrama of it. We were every pair of young and divided lovers there had ever been. We were Romeo and Juliet. We were Abelard and Héloïse, we were Antony and Cleopatra. But we were greater than all of them, because we were real and alive and this was ours. And the secret knowledge of the profound and historic suffering we were forced to endure on account of our love made our separation bearable; it made our separation, I daresay, almost pleasurable. Our sweet, secret pain.

Go ahead, roll your eyes if you want. In this hyperactive age of emails and text messages, the kind of correspondence that Tim and I shared must seem like an anachronism to you. (Anachronism: something so old-fashioned that it's almost ancient.) But I sincerely hope, dear Elizabeth, that someday you might have the pleasure of such an anachronism; that one day you'll experience for yourself the irreplaceable joy of receiving letters from a lover.

This would hardly be a story worth telling if something bad didn't happen next. Something bad did happen—something that put the period at the end of my first semester at Sacred Heart Academy, and that for me will always be the standard by which to measure just how cruel teenage girls can be to one another.

By May of that year I had been at Sacred Heart for four months, and while my affection for the school hadn't grown any, I had settled into a kind of stoic acceptance of my internment. My days were kept especially busy because my parents, to save money, had enrolled me as work-study, which basically meant I was a full-time slave to the nuns. Six o'clock every morning, while the nuns were at chapel, a couple of other hardship students and I went to the kitchen to help Maddy, the cook, prepare breakfast. After that it was: morning bell, lunch, afternoon bell, study hour, help Maddy again, nuns' dinner, girls' dinner, clean up, lights out, sleep. And then again: six o'clock, help Maddy, morning bell, lunch, afternoon bell, study hour . . .

This conventlike regime was amazingly effective in stifling any wayward emotions a girl might have had. Whoever invented it, I thought, must've been a genius. I barely had time to remember how miserable I was.

I'd since become friends with the other charity cases, too: Soo Chee Chong, whose tutoring helped me through Freshman Science; and Anne Harding, whose stiff demeanor hid a bitingly sharp sense of humor that, like her own steely orthopedics, gave us misfortunates the support we needed to carry ourselves upright through the halls of Sacred Heart. During study period, when I wasn't writing letters to Tim, I studied, and my grades gradually began to improve. I received an "A—very nice!" for an essay on *Pride and Prejudice* for Sister Mary Margaret's Freshman Rhetoric—the first A I'd ever received for any essay, anywhere. This pleased my parents, naturally, and validated in their minds their decision to send me to a private Catholic school: they had done the right thing. Those nuns knew their stuff.

Still, in spite of all the sermons in Friday chapel about

turning the other cheek, and in spite of all my mother's efforts to find some reconciliation with me (spring shopping trips to Godchaux's department store in Baton Rouge, for example, or dinner plates that she wrapped for me to bring back to the dorm on Sunday nights), nothing could make me forgive my parents for keeping me and Tim apart. They still refused to let me see or talk to him whenever I took the Greyhound back to Zachary for the weekend. Any kind of reunion was out of the question; it wasn't even mentioned. My parents, of course, knew nothing about the letters—at least not until that May, when the event I'm about to describe to you took place.

It was almost the end of the school year, and despite last-minute anxiety over exams, the halls and classrooms of SHA felt giddy with the prospect of summer. The sun spilled onto the lawns and oaks outside. Squirrels chased each other through the branches, blue jays squawked. Senior boys from Cathedral High, emboldened by their imminent graduation, cruised their cars around the perimeter of the school grounds, luring the more reckless girls to dash across the sidewalks to their windows to exchange notes or kisses or promises.

I was passing through the first-floor hall after lunch hour when I was drawn to the front lobby by some commotion there. A bunch of girls were crowded around the bulletin board opposite the main office, laughing and shoving one another. When I stepped into the lobby one of the girls gasped, "Oh my god," and they all fell silent. A sick, scary feeling coiled up in my stomach. The girls moved aside as I approached, but stayed close enough so they could watch me.

On the bulletin board, pinned up behind the glass in the

middle of the usual announcements about club meetings and lunchtime menus, was a letter from Tim. "Who did this?" I asked, looking around. The only people who ever handled mail at the school, I knew, were the nuns and the Beta Club office assistants. "How'd this get here?" No answer, of course. I turned back to the letter. It was one I hadn't seen yet, dated just two days earlier, and written with even lines on clean white typing paper, as if Tim had taken special care with it. Feeling a dozen pairs of eyes on my back, I scanned the letter.

"Dear Laura My Love," it began. After that I seemed to see only the most private parts, the sentences standing out on the paper as if they were scored in incandescent ink: "We'll find a way to be together again," I read. "Nobody or nothing can keep us apart. Don't you worry." And, "Next time I swear I will hold you and hold you and never let you go. I can't give you up, not that easy. I love you. Don't you know that by now? Haven't I convinced you of that?" On and on it went, each heartfelt sentiment more intimate than the last. "How can you ever think that I'll stop desiring you? I will never stop desiring you. You are the sexiest girl that I ever did know."

I could feel the girls waiting for my reaction to this cruel joke. I could see their reflections in the glass in front of me. I didn't want to give them the satisfaction of seeing me buckle, though, not yet. I tried to open the case, fumbling with the latch, but the thing was locked. I spun around.

"Who did this?" I shouted. "Who?" Some of the girls began backing away, some giggling, some horrified. I saw Anne Harding standing at the rear of the crowd, immobile in her neck brace, wearing a pained, tearful expression. I turned back to wrestle again with the case, but I couldn't get it open, so I hauled back and punched it with the side of my fist. Wedges of glass dropped down inside the wooden case; a large piece crashed to the floor. Someone screamed. I jammed my hand in and grabbed the letter. By now it had become like a hurricane in my ears and eyes and I couldn't hear or see anything clearly. People were jostling, someone was still screaming. I looked down and saw red everywhere. I wondered, distractedly, where it had come from. I watched it spread across my white blouse; I felt it gumming up the floor beneath my penny loafers. Red rosettes blossomed on the letter I held in my hand.

Then Sister Agatha was shaking me: "You will calm down! You will calm right down, miss!"

I protested, shouting back through the noise of the hurricane. "Let me go! I didn't do anything! It was them! They did this! They did it!"

Sister Agatha tried to snatch the letter from my hand—as if somehow the piece of paper was the problem. "You give me that."

"No!" I cried, and grappled with Sister Agatha over the letter, trying to keep it from her, until I did something you should never do to a nun: I hit her. I punched her as hard as I could in the chest and she fell back against the wall. In the next instant, a swarm of hands were on me, dragging me down the hall to the nurse's station.

I suppose by then I was hysterical. But anyone with any sliver of compassion could understand why. The nurse, Ms. Palmer, closed the door and yanked shut the curtains over the corridor windows of the nurse's station. Nuns crowded around, trying to stanch the blood, while Ms. Palmer gave me an injection, "To calm you," she said—as if I were a lunatic in an insane asylum instead of just a hurt, humiliated schoolgirl.

Whatever she gave me worked fast, because soon I was groggy and indifferent to everything. People came and went, class bells rang, phone calls were made. Every time the door opened, a different girl stuck her head in, each face a queer mix of fascination, horror, and pity. "What're you looking at?" I might've asked, but I didn't have the energy or care to speak.

I was shuffled out of the school and into the back of a car. A minute later, I was surprised to find Sister Mary Margaret, Freshman Rhetoric, sitting beside me and holding the bandage to my wrist. Still more surprising, she was stroking my hair and saying, "There, there. It's okay. You'll be fine."

At Baton Rouge General I got six stitches on my left wrist and a shot for tetanus while Sister Mary Margaret held my hand through the entire cloudy, painful operation. I was lying on top of a bed in the recovery room when my parents at last rushed in—my mother blubbery with worry, my father looking faintly ridiculous with stray pieces of straw hanging from the shoulder of his work shirt. Sister Mary Margaret narrated the gentlest possible interpretation of events for them: There had been some accident at the school bulletin board, she said. Nothing too serious—a cut on the wrist, probably two more stitches than were necessary, but better to be on the safe side. Of course, it was difficult being a new student and all, but really, Laura was fine, your daughter was just fine. What she needed now, the good nun said, was rest and sympathy.

You might imagine the gratitude I felt for Sister Mary Margaret. Up until that day I had known her only as a pale older nun who seemed unnaturally preoccupied with grammar; she smelled musty, like a library, and she rustled when she walked, like her very insides were made of parchment. In little more than an hour, though, she had become my new best ally in the world, and a happy disproof to my suspicion that all nuns below their habits were really witches at heart.

The good nun saw me as far as the school dormitory, where mean Sister Hagatha-Agatha took charge again. She and my mother settled me into my room, where I was ordered to stay for two days of bed rest. I mustn't leave the building, I couldn't go to class, and I couldn't have any visitors. Suspended, in other words.

After they'd gone, Melissa looked at me from her bed on the other side of the room. She raised one eyebrow and asked, with something like admiration in her voice, "Wow, what'd you do, cut yourself?"

"Leave me alone."

"Jeez. Only asking."

In the principal's office, meantime, my parents conferred with Principal Evelyn and Sister Agatha. I didn't know then what they were plotting for me; it was only later that I was able to piece together what went on in that meeting. The nuns must have shown my parents the offending letter. My mother, taken in by their severe uniforms and the crosses on the wall, would have broken down and confessed to them the whole ugly truth of why they had brought me to Sacred Heart in the first place: it was on account of that very same pervert boy who had written that very same pervert letter. It was his fault, she said. He had corrupted their daughter and led her to all this, all this . . . perversion. Oh god! What could be done?

To my mother's relief, the nuns knew what to do. They'd had experience in such things. They handed her tissues and, while my father sat by awkwardly, said that the wisest solution would be to confiscate any more of the dangerous evil obscene letters that arrived from the boy. ("Yes. Yes, you're right," I imagine my mother saying, nodding and dabbing her eyes.) The nuns would watch over me at school. And at home during the summer, I should be kept away from the boy and encouraged to take up other activities—softball, say, or sewing. ("Yes, yes, of course, that's what we'll do." "We'll do it!" my father seconded.) Then, when I returned for the fall semester, I would be fully ready to concentrate on my studies. I'd be encouraged to mix with the other girls, join some clubs. That's what I needed. ("Yes, that's what she needs.") They'd seen worse cases, and more often than not, with gentle but firm guidance, the poor lost lamb was brought back into the fold. My mother needn't worry. They'd look after me. They knew what was best. ("Oh, thank you. Thank you so much.")

Oh cruel kindness.

Oh mean charity.

Oh sweet free love.

I still have it, by the way, the scar on the inside of my left wrist. I remember you asked me about it once when you were little. You were sitting in my lap and I was brushing your hair on the back porch one afternoon when you took my hand and ran your finger over the mark. I told you then pretty much the same story that Sister Mary Margaret told my parents at the hospital that day: an accident involving the bulletin board at school, nothing serious, two more stitches than necessary.

Well. Now you know. Today it's pale, almost invisible. But as I'm writing this to you I can turn my wrist up and still see it there, a jagged little memento of my first year at Sacred Heart, and a presage of scars yet to come. But more important than that, it helps to remind me now, Liz, as I wait for you here, of just how hard it is to be your age.

V

Three o'clock now and your father's out on the back porch trying to repair the ceiling fan.

He won't say it, but I can tell he's beginning to get worried. He drove around the city for two hours hunting for you. I suspect that was what finally got to him. "She could be anywhere," he said, throwing the keys down on the counter when he came in. He pulled out your school directory, thinking we might go down the list of your classmates and phone their parents. But with two thousand students we hardly knew where to begin—really, you could be with any of them, or none of them. We gave up after the twelfth call. Then your father thought to phone the school counselor, in case she had some clue as to where you might be, but she wasn't in her office, it being Saturday, and her home phone is unlisted. So after all this, he's on the back porch, taking apart the ceiling fan. I hear him cursing and rattling metal. He'll probably break something soon.

It's been almost fifteen hours, Liz. Fifteen. Do you know how hard this is on your parents? Can you imagine how this makes us feel? Do you even think of us at all?

Missy's parents, you like to say, let her do anything she

wants. Missy's parents let her go out with boys twice her age. Missy's parents let her take vacations with friends to Cancún. Missy's parents let her spend Christmas with her uncle in Aspen. Missy's parents, I would say, are shitty parents. Pardon me, but it's a parent's job, like it or not, to set some boundaries. You're still our daughter, and I honestly feel that we would be failing in our responsibility to you if we let you go off and do whatever you want.

Do I sound like my mother now? Fine. I don't care. Fear and worry, I'm beginning to learn, can turn even the most open-minded person into a raving conservative. I'm ready to send you to your room and lock the door for the rest of your teenage life. You think it's hard being a fifteen-year-old? Just wait until you're the mother of a fifteen-year-old. Honestly, I don't know whether I'll shout at you or hug you when you get back. Probably both.

Okay, I'm going to stop ranting now and make carrot cake. I know it's your favorite, or at least used to be. I've got the TV on in the next room so I can listen to it while I bake. No special bulletins about runaway teenage girls yet. Just the usual dismal reports from Iraq—boys with guns, women in black head coverings crying and shaking their fists at the air.

Those poor women, losing their homes and husbands, their sons and daughters. Mothers all over the world must look at those women and say: I pray to God I'll never have to know that kind of pain.

VI

Have you ever read *The Scarlet Letter*? Do they assign that book in high school anymore? Or is it on some kind of ridiculous banned books list now?

I remembered it while I was shredding carrots. In 1970 the book was on our summer reading list for SHA sophomores. I was back at home in Zachary. My parents still wouldn't let me see Tim, even though he lived just eight miles down the road from us. We were in the same town and yet we might have been stranded on opposite sides of the world. Keeping us apart all this time was worse than unjust: it was cruel. I was fuming over this one night the first week home from school when I pulled out *The Scarlet Letter* from a pile on my desk. Summer reading wasn't due for another three months, but I was so bored and lonely and angry that I dropped down on my bed and began turning pages. And as I kept turning pages, and as my parents creaked around in the front parlor, I got drawn in by the story.

I was amazed. Hester Prynne: she was me! And this Nathaniel Hawthorne, how'd he get to know so much about women? The style was maddeningly long-winded, but the story was so true to life I could hardly believe it had been written over a hundred years ago. I kept turning to the front of the book to check the date.

The cruel New England Puritans were perfect stand-ins for my parents, of course. And poor, brave Hester Prynne, standing up on that scaffold with her baby in her arms and that horrible red letter stuck on her chest—a charity case if I ever saw one. As she was jeered at by the crowd, then scolded by the mean town elders sitting in their balcony, and then banished to a shack at the edge of the village, I couldn't help but think of Tim's letter stuck up on the bulletin board, and of my classmates laughing at me, and of the nuns sending me to my dorm room for a two-day suspension. And yet, even standing on the scaffolding in front of the whole town, Hester managed to hold her head up and look them all in the eye. How did she do that? That's what I wanted to know. How in the world did she get through all that with her pride intact? And if Hester Prynne could do it, I thought, well then, maybe there was hope for me.

Our dog, Tick, barked in the front yard. The windows all around the house stood open, letting in the night air. I heard my father get up and open the front door to scold the dog. "Shush! Shush up!" My mother said something about armadillos. "Crazy mutt," my father said, coming back into the parlor.

Then something clicked against the wall just outside my window. I jerked up in bed, startled. The curtains were parted halfway, the night black and motionless beyond the mosquito screen. I sat listening with the book in my lap. Then again, *click*. Our house had a tendency to creak at night, but nothing like this. Then another click, this one sounding purposeful and directed. I crawled across the bed and peered out the curtains.

Squatting in the shadow of a magnolia tree, just at the edge of the light from my window, was Tim. He held Tick, the dog furiously wagging his tail. I was so happy to see him that a shout escaped my lips. Tick yapped, and Tim signaled for me to be quiet as he tried to calm the dog.

We hadn't seen each other since Christmas, when my father had thrown Tim from the house, so to find him like this now at my window, after all those months of agonized and impassioned letter writing, seemed almost too good to be real. I even began crying a little.

Tim indicated that I should open the screen, and I tried to do so without much noise. The screen was an old one, the kind that hinged at the top and fastened at the bottom, and it hadn't been opened in years. I had to pry the hook loose with a pen. As I was doing this, I heard my father pass through the hallway just outside my door. And seconds later the light suddenly doubled on the lawn as my father switched on the overhead lamp in my parents' bedroom.

Tim crouched closer to the tree trunk, trying to keep to the shadows. Working quietly, he pulled a folded sheet of paper out of his top shirt pocket, unfolded it, and crumpled it into a ball. Seeing what he meant to do, I knelt on my bed and opened the screen as wide as I could, holding it up and away from the windowsill. Tick eagerly watched all of this. Then Tim took aim and lobbed the ball of paper underhanded across the yard and over the boxwood hedge at the side of the house. The ball arced smoothly through the window, bounced off my shoulder, and landed on the rug at the foot of the bed. Tick started barking again. Tim couldn't quiet him—the dog thought we were playing.

I heard my father grousing in the next room, and then he

yanked open the curtains on their window, throwing light like a spotlight onto the side yard.

Tim ducked behind the tree. I could see the shadow of his body standing out along the left side of the trunk. Tick ran back and forth at the tree, barking.

"Hey! Hey!" my father shouted from his window.

"It's okay! I'll get him!" I shouted back, and ran out of my room, past my mother sitting in the parlor watching TV, and down the front porch steps. "Here boy! Come on!" I called, and the dog came running. "It's okay. I got him now!" I shouted, and my father let fall the curtains again on their bedroom window.

Holding Tick in my arms, I lingered on the porch long enough to watch Tim, my brave, clever boyfriend, steal along the edge of the yard, down the side of the gravel drive, and away into the night.

Back in my bedroom, I closed the door and unwadded the note. He knew it was impossible for me to see him because of my parents, Tim had written, but if I could somehow get out Saturday night and come to the Greenwoods Mall, he'd be waiting for me behind the A&W. "I got something important to tell you." He signed it "Love always."

I smoothed the crinkles out of the paper and excitedly folded it into *The Scarlet Letter,* where Hester Prynne sat with her daughter in the cottage at the edge of the village, working her strange and mysterious embroidery as she waited for her redemption, however it might come.

Tim stood up out of the cab of his father's truck as I ran across the parking lot to meet him.

He had begun to grow sideburns and a mustache since his graduation from Zachary High earlier that month, and when we kissed his new hair tickled my nose. Between kisses I told him his mustache made him look like Paul McCartney. He said he didn't like the Beatles, and could I pick someone else? In that case, I said, how about Robert Redford in *Butch Cassidy and the Sundance Kid*? He said that was better, and we went on kissing.

I had fashioned an elaborate lie in order to see Tim that night, telling my parents I was meeting some girlfriends for a movie in town, and then having one of them phone the house so she could casually mention this to my mother, and then studying a review for the movie I had found in the paper just in case I was asked about it. I even begged money from my mother for a Coke and popcorn before I borrowed their car for the night. All of this deceit didn't come naturally to me. I had never lied to my mother before, not in any big way. Lying, I knew, was wrong, and lying to your mother was the very worst kind. It violated the trust that family members are supposed to have for one another. But as far as I was concerned, my mother had already violated that trust when she held me back in the hallway so my father could beat Tim bloody. And anyway, what would she have answered if I'd said I was going to meet Tim that night? She would've said, "No, you're not." So lying to her now, I reasoned, wasn't like lying at all; it was like integrity, a bold act taken for the sake of a higher good.

I don't believe there could have been a more unromantic place in Zachary for our reunion than that patch of black tar behind the A&W. Framing us were the back wall of the drive-in, a Dumpster, a gravel service road, and a weedy vacant lot. The giant neon root-beer mug in front cast a sickly yellow glow over it all. But as with our first meeting almost a year before in the school gym, it hardly seemed to matter where we were. The world was only as big as our bodies, and wrapped up in one another like a blanket around our shoulders, we felt warm and safe and far from our surroundings. Nuzzling Tim's neck, I could smell his father's Old Spice and a piney, earthy scent that made me think of their trailer in the woods. He pulled back and looked at me, fingering my hair and touching the collar of my blouse like there was something amazing there that he had never seen before.

Settling into the cab of the truck, I asked him about his note. "You said it was something important."

He took a deep breath, almost a sigh. "Right." He held my left hand in his lap. "You know how I feel about you," he began seriously, rubbing my fingers. "I've told you before how I see us being together for a long time."

I nodded and watched his eyes. I had a giddy feeling about what was coming.

"I've thought about this a lot. You know we can't start anything until you finish high school. You know that, don't you? You've got to finish high school first."

"I know."

"I'm willing to wait if you are. That's no problem for me."

I kissed his hand. "It's no problem for me, too."

"I want to get myself ready," he said. "I want to feel like I can take care of you, and that I've got something to offer you."

"You do! Don't even worry about that. I don't need anything— "

"Wait, let me finish. You know I've been wondering what I was going to do once I graduated. I wrote you about that, how I've been looking around town and all, but, well . . . there's just not a whole lot of opportunity available for me here. I mean, there's my dad's shop, but you know what that place is like. That's no kind of future.

"So what I decided—and I hope you won't object to this—what I decided to do while we wait for you to finish school is I'm going to enlist."

"You what?"

"Let me explain. I've been talking to a recruiter. He came by on career day— "

"You mean like with the army?" This was not at all what I was expecting. I was picturing something involving a ring, a white veil, and a bouquet of flowers. But this—

"Laura. Listen. Wait a minute. That's what I thought, too. But we got to talking, me and Sergeant Coombs . . ."

Tim laid it all out for me. It had been the last thing on his mind, he said, but if you thought about it, it made perfect sense. The pay, the benefits, the job security. The education. The army would train him—the sergeant said Tim had "officer" written all over him—and when he got out after three years they'd put him through college. I would just be finishing high school then, so it'd be perfect. Hell, even if he did end up in Vietnam, which the sergeant said was not a foregone conclusion, most of the boys there spent half their time sitting on the beach drinking Budweiser beer and eating steak and lobster. "Imagine that," Tim said, amazed. "Budweiser."

As Tim went on, holding my hand and repeating all the nonsense the recruiter had told him, I turned to look out the front windshield of the truck. June bugs swarmed beneath a lamp hanging from a utility pole. Shiny black cockroaches crawled up the back door of the kitchen, and from an exhaust fan a burnt, fleshy smell blew our way across the asphalt. The real world had come back, and with it all its tawdriness. We were just two teenagers sitting in a truck in a grimy back parking lot in Zachary: a skinny fifteen-year-old girl with stringy blond hair and a striped polyester blouse, together with her eighteen-year-old Cajun boyfriend with a scruffy mustache who lived in a trailer with his father and couldn't find a job and so had done what poor boys have done for ages.

Sure, the army has a bad rep these days, Tim was saying, what with Kent State and all. But like the sergeant told him, a smart man could see which way this thing was headed. Already they were cutting back on troops. The whole shebang would probably be over before Tim even got there. He should grab this opportunity while he could because he wouldn't get another chance. And better to enlist now than to get drafted, because then you didn't get any choice at all where they sent you; then you were really screwed. Sign up, and any career he wanted, it'd be his. He liked radios? Fine. They had a school for that. Electrical engineering, medicine, auto mechanics—hell, playing the clarinet—you could do just about whatever you wanted with the army.

I couldn't believe Tim had fallen for all this, and I told him so. "That's nothing but a bunch of crapola. That guy's giving you a line."

"It's true. I got it in writing," Tim said. "It's like a contract."

"You signed it already?"

He nodded. I only had a year of high school, and the only

thing I knew about the war in Vietnam was what I saw on TV, but even I knew it wasn't something any sane person would want to sign up for.

"I can't believe you went and did that!" I said. "The army? My god, Tim. What are you thinking? You can't really be that stupid."

Tim yanked his head back like I'd slapped him. He blinked at me, then turned away and stared out the side window, swallowing.

I felt terrible. I knew how fragile his self-esteem was, and to call him stupid was about the worst thing I could have said. I was reaching to touch his shoulder when he swung back to face me. His eyes were wet with hurt.

"I did it for you!" he cried in a hoarse voice. "Don't you understand? It's for you! It's for you!"

He had done it for me. Even then the idea didn't quite make good sense, but I was only fifteen, as hungry for affection and romance as any fifteen-year-old. I rested my hand on his knee in apology. "Tim. Sweetie. I'm so sorry. I shouldn't have said that." As we slowly began to make up I continued to protest, but feebly. "Of course I don't want you to go," I said. "You could get yourself killed over there!" In the end, though, it didn't take much persuasion for me to see his enlistment as he wanted me to see it, a testament of his love.

He took my hand and kissed the scar on the inside of my left wrist—the scar I'd gotten for him—and pressed it to his heart. I did the same, kissing the palm of his hand—the hand of a soldier now—and laid it solemnly on my chest. Our actions felt weighted with something deeper and more serious than passion. We weren't children anymore; we were adults, in the adult world of war and battle, guns and tanks in faraway foreign countries. My brave soldier boy, risking his life for me! For me!

. . .

Well. That's what it is to be young and stupid, I suppose, isn't it? Boy or girl, you believe anything anyone tells you as long as it's wrapped up in noble-sounding words, and only because you're so desperate not to feel so young and stupid anymore. And in spite of the accumulated wisdom of the ages, this never changes, apparently. I watch those poor, hapless boys on TV marching off to Iraq—because they're nothing more than boys, really, just Tim's age—and I wonder who put them up to this. What can they be thinking?

As for myself, I know how I would answer Tim today. I would say, "Don't you dare do this for me. Don't you dare do that in my name and call it love." Do it for your own dumb ideas of bravery or heroism or patriotism, but please don't say you're doing it for me.

Before I left him that night, Tim stopped and held my face in his hands. As the yellow glow from the root-beer sign seeped into the cab of the truck and the June bugs swarmed beneath the streetlight overhead, he studied my features like he wanted to score them forever in his memory.

The one good thing you can say about war is that it forces you to value the present. It makes you consider last times: this could be the last time I see you. These could be the last words we speak.

"I'll never forget you," he told me.

"I'll never forget you, too," I promised.

You stupid, stupid boy, I would say today. Where did you get the idea this would make me love you more? I loved you regardless.

I'm sure you've seen film clips of the war in Vietnam on TV, Liz. Always alongside the footage of the soldiers fighting in the jungle, you'll see the hippies back home protesting the war: the thousands of long-haired youth marching on the Capitol, burning flags, putting flowers in the barrels of rifles. "Make love, not war," their banners read—a phrase that made my mother click her tongue over her knitting and my father grumble about "disgusting punks."

Seeing those pictures, you might think that the whole country was caught up in the war. But for the girls at SHA in Baton Rouge in 1970, the war in Vietnam was a million miles away. It was no more real for us than *I Dream of Jeannie* or *Gilligan's Island*. The good sons of the good families who sent their daughters to our school didn't go to Vietnam. The good boys who attended Cathedral High School two blocks over didn't go to Vietnam. There was no need to even talk about it. In probably much the same way you feel about the war today, it just wasn't our concern. We had more important things to worry about, things like math tests and school dances and hairstyles. It was only when Tim enlisted that the war began to become real for me, involving real people with real names and actual events.

We had arranged that I would pick up his letters at his father's repair shop in town, and I received the first one two weeks after he left. "Private Prejean now," he wrote. "How do you like the sound of that?" Their drill sergeant at Fort

Benning, Sergeant Millhouse, was a real hard-ass; he'd chew your head off for the slightest little infraction and then make you say how much you loved him. Tim had to do fifty push-ups for not having his razor clean during bunk inspection. "Can you believe that nonsense?" As far as he could tell, the sole purpose of all the rules and regulations—which were the most random bunch of BS you could ever imagine—was to turn new recruits into a pack of nonthinking, nonquestioning, standard-issue remote-control robots whose only purpose in life was to obey and kill. The army didn't even try to disguise this fact, Tim wrote. God help the poor recruit who answered his drill sergeant with "But sir, I thought—" "Did I tell you to think? Did I?" Sergeant Millhouse would scream. "You will not think, you will not wonder, you will not question! You will love me and this army! Do you love me and this army?" "Yes, suh!"

"Craziness," Tim wrote. But at least his company looked out for one another. They were a bunch of good ole boys from farms out west in places like Laramie and Walla Walla and Provo, and towns closer to home, like Natchez and Hattiesburg. He had aced the map-reading tests and navigation runs out in the woods. Turns out he was a pretty good shot with the M14, too. "All that squirrel hunting with my buddies back in Zachary must've paid off, I reckon."

The army, for now at least, didn't sound so bad in Tim's letters. He seemed to enjoy it. Even when he was complaining about it, he seemed to enjoy it.

I wrote back that I was working on a surprise for him for when he came home in a year. This was a scrapbook that I had begun, with the idea that I would gather all the important events of my year together in one place so he wouldn't miss a thing while he was away. I suppose I was too ambitious at first. By the end of the summer my scrapbook was already bulging with pressed flowers, newspaper clippings, movie ticket stubs, Life Saver wrappers. I wanted to share every detail of my life with him, but there wasn't room for every detail.

I puzzled over this while brushing my teeth or fixing my hair in the morning. If you had to choose the moments that best represented your life, what would they be? The small actions that pass almost without our noticing them, yet that we spend most of our time doing: aren't these in fact the real stuff of our lives? Putting on your shoes, eating breakfast, singing songs to yourself, opening and closing doors, racing the dog to the end of the driveway to bring in the newspaper . . .

You could fill all the scrapbooks in the world. The most mundane details of life are not mundane if they're done with someone else in mind. When you're in love, everything's important.

While I wasn't happy to be returning to Sacred Heart for the start of the new school year, I at least found consolation in the fact that I wasn't a freshman anymore. I'd gotten through the worst of it, I figured. I knew which girls to trust, which ones to avoid, and how to please the nuns from time to time with a raised hand and an intelligent-sounding question.

The letters from Tim, though, abruptly stopped coming as soon as I returned to school. I didn't understand it. He had promised to keep writing; he had the school address so there shouldn't have been any problem. After four weeks into the start of the semester with still no word, I became worried for him. What if he had been injured in his training? Or what if he had somehow already shipped off to Vietnam—was even now flying over a jungle and looking down on green palms and thatched huts? Or, worse—and I could hardly bear to let myself think this—what if he was losing interest in me? Already? So soon?

I was fretting over these possibilities one Friday afternoon during study hour when Sister Mary Margaret entered the library. Half looking down at my textbook, half gazing out a window to the side lawn, I barely noticed her dark figure gliding past. She disappeared among the stacks, and two other girls at the far end of the room bent their heads together again in private conversation. I turned back to the green grass and bushes outside—green like they might have had in Vietnam—and resumed thinking about Tim, wondering where he was, hoping he was all right.

After some time there was a soft rustle at my side. I looked up, surprised to find Sister Mary Margaret there.

"Laura," she whispered.

"Sister Mary Margaret," I said. "Hi."

"You're studying?"

"Um . . . yeah." I glanced down at my book. "Chemistry."

"That's good." She looked across the room, then back down at me. She wore a plain wooden cross hanging at the front of her habit. Even though Sister Mary Margaret was one of the senior nuns at Sacred Heart, fifty or sixty years old at least, the wooden cross made her look, somehow, hippielike.

"Do you know this book?" she asked.

I turned my head to read the cover on the dark gray volume she suddenly presented to me. "What is it?"

"*The Letters of Elizabeth Barrett Browning*," she whispered. "We have both volumes. One and two."

"Oh. That's nice."

"You should have a look," she said, laying the book down carefully by my elbow. "I think you'll enjoy it."

"Okay," I said. "Thank you."

"Be sure to put it back when you're finished."

"I will."

"Volume one. Back there—" She indicated the row from where the book had come.

"Right."

"Put it back there. Then you can always find it again later when you need to."

"Thank you, Sister."

She smiled oddly as she moved off, her habit waving. "Enjoy."

These nuns, I thought: too much prayer and no sex. They were all a little loony.

I had to go soon to my job in the kitchen. I began to gather my things, but just to please Sister Mary Margaret, I slid the Elizabeth Barrett Browning toward me. The book didn't look like it got much use at SHA; it was as old and dusty as the sister herself. But then as I picked it up, the pages fell open on a letter. The envelope was addressed from Fort Devens, Massachusetts, to me, care of Sacred Heart Academy.

In an instant I understood: the nuns had been keeping my mail from me. I remembered the incident with the bulletin board last spring, and the meeting my parents had in the principal's office. They had arranged it all then, their scheme to protect me from the corrupting influence of Tim's letters. But Sister M&M, that crafty old grammarian, had somehow managed to intercept Tim's letter in the front office so that she could secretly pass it on to me.

I felt silly with happiness. Like a spy, I glanced around the library and snuck the letter into my satchel. I didn't want to read it in public; I was afraid I might burst out singing. Before I left the library, I slid the volume back into its place on the shelf with a note inside for Sister Mary Margaret: "Thank you thank you thank you thank you."

After that, every Friday, I would check the stacks. And more often than not, there in volume 1 of *The Letters of Elizabeth Barrett Browning* would be a letter from Tim. Sister Mary Margaret and I never said a word about it. But sometimes when I passed her in the hallway, her hands tucked into the folds of her habit, the oversized wooden cross swaying on her chest, she would nod and smile at me in a sly, conspiratorial manner.

. . .

Do you know Elizabeth Barrett Browning, by the way? Do girls read her in high school anymore? In case you don't, here's a little background for you, some things I gleaned while looking from time to time through volume 1. You especially, dear Liz, might find it interesting.

When Elizabeth Barrett began her exchange of letters with the famous Scottish poet Robert Browning, she was already forty years old, an invalid living with her parents in London. Their letters led to friendship, which led to love.

Elizabeth's father was so mean and jealous, though, that he wouldn't accept the idea of marriage for his daughter. And so she eloped, brave thing. One morning in September she stole out of the house with her maid, met Robert in a waiting carriage, and fled with him to Italy, never again to return to her home in England. While in Italy she finally showed Robert her "Sonnets from the Portuguese," written for him during their early correspondence. I know that at least a couple of lines from one of them are familiar to you. We had to memorize the poem that year in Sister Mary Margaret's class. It's addressed from a woman to her lover, but I always thought it could as well be from a mother to a child. This is it, Sonnet 43:

How do I love thee? Let me count the ways.
I love thee to the depth and breadth and height
My soul can reach, when feeling out of sight
For the ends of Being and ideal Grace.
I love thee to the level of everyday's
Most quiet need, by sun and candlelight.
I love thee freely, as men strive for Right;
I love thee purely, as they turn from Praise.
I love thee with the passion put to use
In my old griefs, and with my childhood's faith.
I love thee with a love I seemed to lose
With my lost saints,—I love thee with the breath,
Smiles, tears, of all my life!—and, if God choose,
I shall but love thee better after death.

You could have done worse than to have been named after a nineteenth-century Romantic poet, Liz. Imagine if Sister Mary Margaret had hidden Tim's letters in a volume of Homer. You might be named Penelope, or Athena, or Clytemnestra.

From his letters I learned that after boot camp Tim had been sent to Fort Devens for advanced training. He had never been north of the Mason-Dixon Line before, so everything about New England struck him as novel: the tidy red barns and white churches, the old neighborhoods and cracked sidewalks, the way people walked their dogs on leashes and never said hello, only nodded their heads with their lips pressed shut when you passed them on the street.

At Fort Devens he was enrolled in Intelligence School. "Apparently *someone* thinks I'm smart," he wrote. He was studying telecommunications, and already knew more about band waves and signal codes than he ever wanted to. "I thought I finished with books once I left high school. That appears not to have been the case." Suddenly he found himself in a laboratory with a bunch of guys in eyeglasses trying to decipher circuit diagrams. One of his instructors said he had a real aptitude for electronics. "Like father, like son I guess." He and his bunkmate put together the wackiest hi-fi set you could imagine using spare parts swiped from the radio lab and a chassis they made out of tin cans, forks, and a serving tray from the canteen. "Most surprising thing was, when we turned it on, it worked. We can pick up Casey Kasem on WABC from New York. How do you like that?" he wrote. And so on.

As happy as I always was to receive Tim's letters, that semester I was also beginning to discover my own aptitudes. At the urging of Sister Mary Margaret I had joined the staff of the school newspaper, *The Beacon*. The first article I ever wrote was an interview with Maddy, the school cook I helped in the kitchen. Maddy was an amazingly cheerful fifty-year-old black woman who had come to work for the nuns when she was just a teenager. I titled the piece "Silent Heroes: Maddy Simms, Thirty-three Years at SHA and Still Smiling."

My article struck everyone as being supremely principled and humane—which, as I remember, hadn't been my intention at all, but I welcomed the praise just the same. Girls I had never spoken to, juniors and seniors, stopped me in the hallway to thank me for my bravery in exposing the hypocrisies and racial injustices occurring *right here at SHA*—injustices that, as far as I was concerned, were basic facts of life and had never needed exposing to anybody. But no matter. I clipped the article and set it aside, with the idea that I would add it to my scrapbook for Tim as soon as I found the time.

Because after the success of my first article, I became extremely busy with the newspaper. The editor, Kim Cortney, appointed me as special features editor, which basically meant that I was called upon to write anything, anytime. I began to spend all my free periods in the newspaper office, a cramped four-desk room in a hallway near the gym. I learned how to write a proper lead and how to estimate column length for a mock-up. I also learned that we girls from the newspaper club had a surprising degree of freedom on campus. We could come and go pretty much as we pleased. All you had to do was say, "Got a deadline, Sister," wave a piece of paper in the air, and they'd let you pass.

"So good to see you mixing with the other girls," Principal Evelyn said, nodding smugly as she stood watch outside her office door.

One Friday at the end of the semester, the newspaper club was excused from class to attend, unchaperoned, a daylong Scholastic Press Association conference at Louisiana State University. Since becoming a boarder at Sacred Heart I'd rarely left the school, so I was thrilled to be invited. I rode with Kim, who had her own car, a racy, sky-blue Capri with white bucket seats. As she drove she sang along to "Bridge Over Troubled Water," puffing on a cigarette and blowing the smoke out a crack in her window. I watched from the backseat, awestruck by her cool. On the last chorus she threw her arm out, belting the song melodramatically with the other girls in the car until I had to laugh aloud.

Arriving at LSU, the club veterans took a few minutes to preen before leaving the car. I borrowed a lipstick and brush and did the same. "Boys," Kim said, checking herself in the mirror of her compact, "don't really care about how well you can write a lead. What they care about . . . are your lips. How do I look?"

We spent the day in workshop sessions moderated by passionate LSU journalism students and bearded young professors. They quoted John Locke, Alexander Hamilton, and Hunter S. Thompson, talking about the sacred power of the word, and the beauty of simple, honest prose, and the journalist's moral duty to uphold the freedom of the press. After the conference was over, we ended the day at an Italian restaurant near LSU's campus with a bunch of boys from the Cathedral High School paper. We all tumbled into the padded red booths, fired with a newfound sense of self-importance as newspaper writers. Who'd ever thought that what we were doing was so crucial to the well-being of civilization? Who'd ever thought something as simple as words on paper could change the world? Looking around the table at my classmates that evening under the glow of a low-hanging lamp, I imagined I could see in them, like an aura burning around their shoulders, the potential for greatness.

Sitting across from me was the photographer from the Cathedral High newspaper, a boy named Charles Benton—"Chip." I'd seen him before at pep rallies and school functions, lurking at the edges of the scene with his camera. A fair boy with a goofy smile and tight curly hair that fitted like a bushy helmet on his head, he was almost indistinguishable from half the other boys at CHS, who were, by and large, polite, dull, middle-class Southern teenagers. Armed with his camera, though, Chip became bold and full of purpose.

I'd been so sheltered at Sacred Heart that the last boy to flirt with me was Tim, on the night we'd met at the Freshman-Senior Get Acquainted Dance in Zachary. So when Chip began making jokes at my expense, and overusing my name, and generally acting like a pest for most of the day, I hardly recognized what he was doing.

"He likes you," Kim had said, pulling me aside during the conference.

"Who? Chip? You've got to be kidding."

"Oh my god. He's nuts about you."

Now at the restaurant, even before we ordered Cokes, he uncapped his camera and started taking pictures of me across the table. He narrated the whole time, too, as if imagining the captions that would appear under the photos in *Life* magazine.

"Laura Jenkins seen relaxing with her society friends at the world-famous Little Italy in Baton Rouge. Laura Jenkins sips her water through a straw."

"You're wasting your film," I said.

"Laura Jenkins screws up her face in annoyance at the paparazzi who trail her every move."

"You're impossible."

"Laura Jenkins—Hey!—throws a napkin at the hapless young photographer who ducks out of the way at the last minute. Missed me!"

Before the evening was over, and two large pizzas and several pitchers of Coke later, we girls from SHA had made enthusiastic promises to collaborate more frequently with the boys from the CHS newspaper. They would help us, we would help them. Sharing resources, cross-campus exchanges, regular visits to one another's staff rooms—that kind of thing.

"I am so psyched," Kim said back in her car. Never mind the newspaper. Visits to the CHS campus were about the most thrilling thing a SHA girl could wish for. "You walk down the hallway between their classes and, oh my god, it's like you're Marilyn Monroe or something. The boys positively drool."

"I'll send you prints!" Chip shouted from his car as he pulled away in the parking lot. "Signed!"

"You do that!" I shouted back.

"Told you," Kim said, punching in the cigarette lighter on her dash. "He's crazy about you."

. . .

I tripped up the stairs to my room, feeling light-footed and happy, like I was drunk from too much Coke and pizza. I thought, in a flush of amazement, that maybe the way I was feeling now was the way high school girls were *supposed* to feel. Did girls like Kim Cortney feel this way all the time? And why shouldn't I? Hadn't I as much right as anybody to be happy?

Rounding the corner of the corridor, I ran into my roommate, Melissa, standing at the hallway telephone. She was holding the receiver, looking annoyed.

"Okay, never mind, here she is," she said into the phone. She thrust it at me. "Finally. He's been calling every half hour."

I took the phone. "Tim?"

"Laura? Where you been? Honey. I been trying to call you all night. I got . . . Where you been?" He sounded upset, or drunk, or both.

"Nowhere," I said. "I mean, a conference. A newspaper conference. With some people. What's wrong? Are you okay?"

"I'm leaving. Shipping out."

"You're leaving? To where?"

"Where do you think? Vietnam."

Vietnam? It seemed too soon. Hadn't he just started training? What about the intelligence school and all that? The radio classes?

But no, he was right on schedule. He'd been at basic training nine weeks, seventeen weeks at advanced. Only thing was, he told me, they weren't giving him any leave time. His unit had special orders to ship out ASAP, direct from the base.

"I don't want to go. I miss you so much. Honey, honey. Where you been?"

"Oh—I miss you, too. When do you have to go?"

"Tomorrow. I went out and got something for you. I did it for you."

"What'd you do?"

"It's right . . . Ouch." There was a clunk, like he'd dropped the phone. "Got it right here," he resumed. " 'Laura.' It's all bloody and shit now. Not supposed to look at it."

"What?"

"Tattoo."

"Oh, no. Oh, Tim. No."

"Yep. Got it right here. Inside my rifle arm. Every time I turn it up to shoot, I can see your name."

"What'd you go and do something like that for?"

"For you! I did it for you. You don't like it?"

"You didn't have to do that."

"But I love you. I love you, Laura. Do you love me?"

"Oh, honey. Of course I do. You know I do."

"It's permanent. Won't ever come off. Won't ever have to."

"Oh, Tim."

"I won't ever forget you."

"I won't ever forget you, either."

"Laura, Laura. You're gonna wait for me come home?"

"Of course I will."

"Say you'll wait for me."

"I'll wait for you."

A beeping noise sounded through the line. "Shit. I don't have no more change. Laura!"

"I'll write you."

"Promise?"

"I promise. Tim—!"

And then there was silence: black silence, that in the moments as I gripped the phone seemed to grow deeper and deeper until it was black as the dark spaces between stars.

VII

The carrot cake is done and sitting in the center of the table, waiting for you.

I finally spoke to Missy DeSalle about an hour ago. It turns out she and her friends haven't left for Florida yet; they're going tomorrow morning. And yes, she says, you talked about joining them, but she hasn't heard from you since yesterday. "Don't worry, Laura, I'm sure Liz'll be just fine," Missy said before we hung up. "She probably just wants some time to herself. Be patient."

"When I want your advice, I'll ask for it, you dumb little tramp," I wanted to say, but held my tongue. I don't trust that girl. I bet she knows more than she's letting on. She sounds like an expert in making up stories for parents, thoughtlessly babbling lies as she fluffs her hair before going out for the night in that extravagant little Mercedes of hers. No wonder she's so popular.

I couldn't sit still anymore, so I took a break from writing and went for a walk around the neighborhood. The local kids, delirious with the start of a whole week of spring vacation, were out playing tag in the street before dinnertime, running across yards and sidewalks, shouting and laughing, heedless of everything. I resented their joy. It seemed like an affront to all my worry. How could they run and shout like that when you're missing? I bit my lip and walked on, shutting out the thought of an end too painful to allow.

I turned my attention down to the ground. I began studying the crabgrass overtaking the edge of the sidewalk, and peered into the weeds and black water sloughing in a ditch beside the road, imagining that, like some TV detective, I might find a clue that would tell me where you've gone—a scarf, maybe, or a scrap of paper, a plastic hair barrette. I tried to tally up all the evidence that could explain your disappearance. The hushed phone conversations on the back porch, for instance, or that boy's jeep parked in front of the house, or the tears I thought I saw as you came running in one night over the Christmas holiday . . .

I spotted something glinting in the weeds. Stepping down into the ditch, I sifted through the overgrown grass until I found a Coke can. But then standing there on the slope of the ditch, one foot up, the other foot down, staring at the dirty can in my hand, I stopped myself. A Coke can. What was I doing? This was crazy. I dropped the can back into the ditch, brushed off my hands, and resumed walking.

Rounding the corner up on Hyacinth, I fell to reminiscing. You probably don't remember when we first moved here thirteen years ago. You were only two then, just beginning to talk. It suddenly struck me that this neighborhood will be the place you'll remember forever as home. When people ask you thirty years from now "Where are you from?" this is what you'll think of. Right here, this is your world. It was on this very street where you learned to ride your first bike. I remember you liked this stretch of pavement because it was flat and easy with grass on either side. And the house up there on the left: that was where the Fields' pet terrier got out one Halloween night and chased you screaming back to your daddy's arms. And here, nearer our home, was the very place on the sidewalk where you slipped on a patch of ice one freezing winter day and had to get three stitches in the back of your head. You were more upset about bleeding all over your new Christmas coat than you were about the cut. How old were you then? Five? Six? Not that long ago, really.

I stopped off at the Banards' next door to let them know what's happened. They haven't seen anything, of course, but they promised to keep an eye out. And just now, after I got in, your father went out with the car again, "Just to have a look." We agreed that one of us should stay at home in case you call. I've got the TV back on, listening to the early evening news.

We're grabbing at straws here, Elizabeth. Your dad driving around in the Buick, me writing this interminably long letter. But what else can we do? There's nothing we can do. I keep going back to a line from that poem by your namesake, about "my old griefs" and "my childhood's faith." Waiting for you, writing this letter, I feel like I'm teetering between those two sentiments, a pessimism born of experience and a desperate hope born of helplessness. In dredging up all these old griefs from my past, I cling to the thought that this act itself will somehow create a better future for both of us, that with these words I'll weave a charm that will spell our reconciliation and draw you home.

For times of doubt and trouble, the nuns at Sacred Heart prescribed prayer. We even had special rosary services before important exam dates. God, we were told, would always hear and answer our prayers, no matter how big or small they were. There was a caveat, however, a kind of special exemption that the nuns told us about, one that always infuriated me, and that never failed to put my childhood's faith to the test. And this was that, yes, God would always answer our prayers, but maybe not in the ways we expected or even wanted.

Well. I want to finish this letter before you get home. And then we'll have dinner and cake, and things will begin to get better for us, you'll see. I promise.

VIII

Tim couldn't believe the Christmas dinner he was treated to when he arrived in Vietnam. He was stationed at a scrubby base camp up in the hills in the middle of nowhere, and yet on Christmas day a giant double-rotor Chinook helicopter magically descended from the clouds to deliver full turkey dinners to all 120 boys at the camp. They had corn bread dressing, cranberry sauce, sweet potatoes, shrimp cocktail . . . "Shrimp cocktails! Where the heck did they get shrimp cocktails?" Tim wrote.

And just as the recruitment sergeant had promised, there was Budweiser beer, all you could drink. Hell, they even had a bar right there on base, with Vietnamese girls in shiny long dresses and pigtails serving martinis. Scruffiest bunch of soldiers you could ever imagine, and their hooches nothing but falling-down shacks propped up with sandbags, but he wasn't complaining, not yet. More than anything he was looking forward to getting out and seeing some of the countryside. As radio intelligence, his missions were strictly top secret, so he wasn't allowed to say when and where he was going exactly, but he'd write me as often as he could. And where were the letters I promised him, by the way? I had his address now so there wasn't any excuse.

"I keep thinking back on that night," he wrote. "Hard to believe it was only a year ago. Already seems like ten. But when I close my eyes I can remember like it was yesterday. I see your white skin on the rug, and the firelight glow on your hair, and that soft look in your eye when you told me you love me. I swear, it's the one thing that keeps me going. I'm sure glad I got you back home waiting for me. You'll always be the number one girl for me, Laura Jenkins. Now write!"

That spring at Sacred Heart, meanwhile, I was finally beginning to feel myself more a part of the school. To be sure, I still had little in common with the well-bred Catholic girls who were my classmates. But over time people can adapt to almost anything, I suppose. Even prisoners begin to feel at home.

My fitting in had to do mainly with my work on *The Beacon*. I'd begun a series of profiles on SHA personalities called "Spotlight On . . . !" Kim gave me half the third page to write about whomever I wanted, and for the first time in my life I felt what it's like to wield some power. Girls who had never before been nice to me now smiled and said hello in the hallways. Faculty took me aside to give me subtle and not-so-subtle suggestions about which teacher or student would be a good subject for my next profile. I hadn't written about Principal Evelyn yet, Sister Agatha reminded me. She had a very interesting background. Why not interview her? Surely she deserved a profile.

But I ignored all their suggestions and turned instead to my truest allies at the school, the charity cases. Over lunch in the cafeteria, I interviewed Soo Chee Chong, the quietest girl on campus. Who ever knew that Soo spoke fluent Mandarin? Or that she had ended up in Baton Rouge, of all places, because her parents, both prominent university professors back in Beijing, had fled the Cultural Revolution to avoid being killed by the Red Guards? If they didn't like you, Soo said, the soldiers would just walk up to you in the street and shoot you in the face. The whole family had made a lucky escape through Taiwan, smuggled across the strait in the bottom of a fishing boat, which was why to this day, Soo said, she couldn't stand the smell of raw fish. Her name in Chinese, she told me, meant "the beautiful sound of jade."

Anne Harding, after years of surgery and doctor's visits, turned out to be an expert on scoliosis. The piece I wrote about her, "Profile in Courage," dwelt on current medical treatments for curvature of the spine and what could be done to prevent it. Curvature, Anne explained, was measured in degrees of variance from the vertical. At eighteen degrees, hers was considered a mild curve and could be corrected with bracing in 90 percent of the cases. If left untreated, however, the deformity could worsen, twisting the chest until the ribs jutted to one side, the breasts and hips became uneven, and one shoulder tilted up high toward the ear. Every teenage girl should be checked annually for curvature of the spine, Anne said, which led to a rush on Nurse Palmer's office the week the piece was printed.

And in my profile on Christy Lee, the near-invisible lone black student in our sophomore class, she revealed how she had managed to trace her family roots all the way back to the Ivory Coast of Africa, and a slave trader named Captain Burt Keenan who had sold her great-great-great-grandfather, branded and chained, to a plantation owner in Charleston for two thousand dollars—which, Christy pointed out, was actually a high price to pay for a man in those days. Christy provided the title herself for that piece: "Let Freedom Ring."

The charity cases seemed to become a little less shy after their articles were published, a little less bitter. Girls would stop at our lunch table to get Soo Chee Chong to write their names in Chinese characters on the front of their notebooks. From time to time I even saw Anne Harding laughing aloud in the hallway, her chin bobbling against her neck brace. The journalism students at LSU had been right. There was power in writing. Words held magic that could transform people.

That spring, too, Chip Benton started to become a regular at our tiny newspaper staff office. He was always dropping off photos of CHS events we might use, or offering us extra bottles of toner solution. We had our own school photographers, of course, but Chip was such a good-natured fellow, and his curly helmet of hair was so cute—and he was a boy, after all, which was such a weird novelty at SHA—that we were always happy to have him around.

And true to his word, he gave me signed prints of the photos he took of me that night at the Italian restaurant. He'd blown them up and developed and cropped them in such a way that they looked moody and evocative, like stills from a 1950s black-and-white movie, or celebrity nightclub photos from an era more glamorous and richly lived than our own. They were gorgeous, really—funny and profound, silly and tender all at once. I kept them in a desk drawer in my dorm room. I didn't dare put them up on the walls—they seemed too intimate, somehow—but from time to time I took them out to admire them.

I was adapting so well to life at Sacred Heart that year, in fact, that I hated to return to Zachary for the summer. But once the school year ended and the dorm shut down, we boarders had no choice. I packed all my belongings into boxes again and moved back home, where a kind of silent truce prevailed between me and my parents. I'd decided that as long as I had to live with them I would be polite, nothing more. My personal life was my own business from now on; I wasn't going to risk sharing anything with them ever again. When they asked how things were going at school, I'd say, "Fine." At dinner, it was "Pass the butter, please" and "Thank you." My father hardly seemed to notice this dearth of communication. My mother, though, more attuned, would stop by my room after dinner.

"Is everything all right, Laura?"

"Yes."

"Are you enjoying your summer?"

"Yes."

"Well . . ." She watched me a moment longer from the doorway, her dark eyes twitching in their sockets. "Nice to have you back. Good night."

"Night."

Listening to her steps creaking down the hallway from my room, I could feel the distance between us growing, and I wondered if this distance would grow so great that eventually, passing through opposite doors of the parlor or brushing shoulders on the way to and from the bathroom, we might be no more familiar to one another than strangers at a bus station, bound for different destinations.

Every week or so, I went alone to Jack Prejean's shop to check for mail from Tim. That was our arrangement: during the school year, Tim would write to me at SHA, and during the summer, he'd write care of his dad's shop in town.

"Got one right here," Jack would say, turning around to pick up a letter from his desk behind the counter. I could tell he looked forward to my visits. While I sat in a chair to read Tim's news, Jack leaned on the counter watching me, the sun angling in through the junked TVs and radios piled on shelves against the shop window. If I laughed aloud or otherwise reacted in some way, he snapped up his eyebrows. "What? What'd he say?" Then we would share what we knew of Tim and his life in Vietnam, which, in the letters that came that first summer, still sounded like one big Boy Scout adventure.

He'd been assigned to an airmobile radio research team, Tim wrote. He figured he wasn't revealing any army secrets to tell us his job basically entailed him and another guy driving out into a field with a radio mounted on a jeep to try and locate enemy transmitters. "Translate that to me sitting hunched over the receiver all day while Patterson, a guy who's got one more patch on his shirt than me, lies in the hammock strumming his guitar and getting a suntan." While they were out snooping on the North Vietnamese Army, they lived off Coca-Cola and C rations, which weren't so bad really after you heated them up on the exhaust manifold of the jeep. Franks and beans for dinner, bananas cooked in their skins with Hershey chocolate for dessert. Sleeping out under the stars—just like camping out. Most times it was hard to believe there was even a war on. Everywhere you looked it was just farms and fields and dirt roads, with little kids who followed you around like ducks, and everything quiet as a Sunday afternoon in Zachary. Only difference was, in Zachary you didn't have choppers flying overhead, or military convoys tearing past, or firefights that boomed and lit up the night sky over the hills like thunder and lightning before a hurricane. Lucky for him he never had to get too close to the fighting; they just hung back and diddled with their radios. He hadn't even fired his rifle yet, which was just fine with him, Tim wrote, because then he'd have to take it apart and clean it, which was a real pain in the A.

Jack chuckled, shaking his head. "Man oh man. Army life sure seems to suit the boy, doesn't it?"

Sometimes Jack and I scribbled responses to Tim on the back of a repair order form, trading wisecracks in writing. "You better get on home. Your girl's got a dozen beaux circling her!" Jack wrote.

"Don't listen to Jack," I wrote below that. "Your girl doesn't have any beaux circling her. But she does miss you and wish you were here. Be safe."

At times like these I felt closer to the Prejeans than to my own family, and was reminded of why I fell in love with Tim in the first place. His life seemed so honest and simple that a girl couldn't help but want to be a part of it.

. . .

The big surprise that summer, though, had nothing to do with Tim and the war in Vietnam. It was a phone call. One sleepy afternoon my mother hollered for me to come quick to the kitchen.

"It's a boy," she said when I came through the doorway, her face a screwed-up look of expectancy and sourness. After I took the phone, she stood there watching.

"Laura?"

"Who's this?"

"Chip."

I glared at my mother until she left the kitchen. Then I turned toward the wall so I could talk, my heart beating a little faster than it should have been.

Chip had run into Kim Cortney in town the day before and thought he'd give me a call. A bunch of them from school were planning to get together at his house that Friday night, he said—no big deal, shoot some pool, hang out, maybe go swimming. He knew it was a long drive from Zachary, but hey, if I was in town . . .

He gave me directions. A big white house right on LSU lake, easy to find. Didn't matter if I couldn't play pool, he said. He'd teach me. No charge.

That'd be great, I told him. Wow. Okay. Sure. I just had to ask my parents first.

"Okay, so . . . great. See you Friday," he said.

"See you Friday."

"Great."

"Great!"

I had never been invited to a party in Baton Rouge, much less to a party involving swimming and billiards. I pictured the evening as a scene out of *Gone with the Wind,* with plantation-sized houses and elegant Southern girls sweeping down curved stairways in green gowns, while the men—Chip looking debonair in a gray tailcoat—leaned against the mantel in the billiard room sipping bourbon. With this one phone call, Chip had reached down his hand to snatch me up into a world of privilege and ease, a universe away from the dull family farms and bleak trailer parks of Zachary. I felt a little like Cinderella, or whatever the Southern version of her would be. At dinner that night I asked my parents if I could go.

"See what your father thinks," my mother said.

"You want to what?" my father asked, barely looking up from his fried liver and onions.

"Borrow the car to drive to Baton Rouge for a party."

"Don't think so," he said, and went back to eating.

"Mom?" I pleaded.

She shrugged. "If your father says no—"

I stared at her, this pinch-faced stranger sitting a hundred miles away at the end of the table who nonetheless wielded absolute power over me, who with a word could send me to a convent school in another city or deny me the chance to attend the most important party I'd ever been invited to, one that had the potential to change my life forever.

I couldn't contain myself. "You're useless. You know that?" I cried. "Useless! What good are you as a mother? You're nothing. You don't do anything. You just sit there and agree with whatever he says. You don't help me, you don't care, you don't . . . I never get to go to parties! I never go anywhere!" I threw down my napkin and left the table.

"You come back here and apologize, young lady!" my father shouted, his mouth full of potatoes.

"I hate living in this house!" I yelled, slamming my bedroom door.

. . .

Sound familiar, Liz? It does to me. In fact, I'm ashamed at how familiar it sounds. I didn't curse my parents and steal their car and leave, but I sure wanted to.

That was the night when, crying furiously in my room, I promised myself I would never treat my daughter the way my mother treated me. No, that would never happen. Because my daughter and I, I swore, would be best friends. We'd laugh and gossip. I'd give her advice about boys, and she'd tell me when my clothes were beginning to look frumpy and old-fashioned. When her father said no, I'd take her aside, slip a few dollars into her hand, and tell her not to worry, she should go ahead and enjoy herself.

As it turns out, Liz, we talk about as little as my mother and I did, don't we? You huff and frown whenever I ask you to take out your earphones, and if I dare try to broach personal matters with you, you groan like I'm hurting you. Just like I did, you keep your private life locked up tight in a cupboard, hiding it from the one person who most wants to help you.

Am I really that bad? As bad as my own mother? I don't feel like a villain, and yet you probably see me that way: a mean old witch whose only aim is to keep you from having any fun in life. But as hard as it may be to believe, your father and I really do have your best interests at heart. We might screw up now and then—we're only human, after all—but we don't set out to be cruel. I don't think any parent does.

If I could speak now to my teenage self, I might tell her to be more forgiving of her parents. Maybe they were doing the best they could. It's possible. If adulthood has taught me anything, it's that even grown-ups are fallible. We're not a whole lot smarter than we were when we were teenagers.

We still feel the same stir of emotions, the same awkward human needs and doubts we felt then. Only the shell grows thicker; the inside, the more tender parts, remains surprisingly unchanged. Often—and this is a secret that not many parents will tell their children—often, we don't know what the hell we're doing. And so we yell, we shout, we slap our children.

We still make mistakes, daughter. Oh yes, all the time.

"Avoid sentimentality at all costs," Sister Mary Margaret used to warn us.

An odd rule coming from her, I always thought, considering Sister M&M was about the most sentimental nun you could imagine, welling up any time she read two lines of poetry aloud to us. But it was a good rule, I suppose, for a classroom full of teenage girls whose confused emotions always churned just below the surface of their thin skin, threatening to spill over at the least agitation.

Back at school my junior year, I stopped by the library one Friday afternoon late in the fall semester and found a letter in the usual place, volume 1 of Elizabeth Barrett Browning. I remember standing between the shelves, my satchel on my shoulder, as I opened the thin airmail letter and began reading.

Perhaps it shouldn't have come as too much of a surprise to learn that Tim had decided to stay on for another tour of duty in Vietnam. He explained how the extra combat pay plus cost-of-living allowance would add up to a nice savings. The army had him one way or the other for the next two years, he wrote, so he might as well take advantage of it. To sweeten the deal—and this was the big news he wanted to tell me—he had just been awarded a lateral promotion to corporal. For the first time in his life, people were saluting him and calling him "sir." "Don't worry, I won't make you salute me when I get home," he joked.

But most important, he finally felt he was doing something useful with his life, helping the South Vietnamese defeat the Communists. Pull out now, he said, and the whole thing would fall apart. No matter what the protestors back home said, and no matter all the horror stories you heard on the news, he knew that what they were doing in Vietnam was for the better. . . .

When I finished reading, I stuffed Tim's letter in my satchel, not quite wanting to think about it yet, and hurried to the gym, where preparations were under way for the Winter Formal. I was on the planning committee and was supposed to be overseeing decorations. The other girls were already there, putting up the backdrop for the souvenir photos and weaving crepe paper streamers. I dropped my satchel and threw myself into the work. Our theme that year was "Winter Nights," and so the inside of the school gym was supposed to somehow look like, well, a winter night.

"The stars?" a freshman named Amy asked, holding out a stack they'd finished wrapping with aluminum foil. I showed her how we'd hang them from the ceiling with fishing line, assuring her that with the distance and the dim light her cardboard stars would look twinkling and gorgeous, not at all stupid. We rolled out the giant gym ladder and peered up into the rafters, wondering how we'd go about it—

And yet despite all the busyness and chatter around me,

I couldn't help but think of Tim. I was reminded of a dance two years ago at Zachary High, when I was a freshman and he was a senior. It seemed like half a lifetime ago already.

"But soon you'll graduate and I'll be home and we can finally settle down," he'd written in his letter to me. "Maybe next time you're back in Zachary you can begin looking at neighborhoods you like." He'd put his daddy to work, too, checking out home prices. Wasn't any reason we couldn't take out a loan and move into someplace nice. Other fellas threw all their paychecks away on fancy cars and what have you, but Tim was saving all his for me and him together. Heck, with the money he earned he might be able to turn around his daddy's shop yet, expand it to home stereo sales. That's where the real business opportunities were—

"Sound check!" Christy Lee shouted from the wings of the stage, and all at once the gym filled with loud, lush music. Christy ran out from behind the curtains and slid to a stop in the center of the basketball court. She began miming the song.

I say to myself, "You're such a lucky guy."
To have a girl like her is truly a dream come true.

The other girls clapped and cheered her on. Then Christy ran over and tugged my arm. I protested—I was busy, I didn't know the song, she should get somebody else.

"Come on!" she said, and dragged me out onto the floor. I reluctantly fell into step beside her for a silly Jackson 5 dance routine. She called the moves: slide, kick, turn, and back.

But it was just my imagination
Running away with me . . .

"Boy in the house!" someone shouted, and then I saw, over Christy's shoulder, Chip Benton. He was standing in the door of the gym, grinning. He raised his camera and slinked toward us, snapping off pictures.

"SHA girls seen busily preparing for the annual Winter Formal," he narrated. "Here they are practicing dance steps, hoping to impress boys. SHA student council secretary Laura Jenkins shows off her funky moves."

"Out! Out!" the girls yelled, throwing crepe paper at him. Christy, laughing, spun me in his direction. He held his camera aside as I thumped into his chest. "Oof."

"If you insist," Chip said. He lowered his camera, took my hands, and began to dance with me. My classmates cheered and oohed.

"You dance divinely," Chip said.

"You're crushing my fingers," I answered. Luckily, the record was reaching its end. "Oops, sorry," I said. "Song's over. Too bad."

But Chip held tight, because Christy had disappeared behind the stage curtains and restarted the record.

"Oops, too bad. It's playing again," Chip said. "It'd be very rude to leave me now."

Then Christy threw the switch that cut the overhead flood lamps, and suddenly we were at the Winter Formal, the gym floor bathed in blue and silver lights. As the song played again, the other girls paired up and turned in couples around us, singing along in their high, hopeful voices beneath the cut-out stars and artificial moonlight:

Ooh-hoo-hoo-hooh,
Soon we'll be married
And raise a family . . .

"You really do dance well," Chip said. "I'm not kidding."

"I guess you do, too," I said. His right hand rested sure but easy in the middle of my back, his left hand cupped warmly around mine. He pulled me closer and rested his chin on top of my head while the Temptations sang about building a little home out in the country with two or three children, just like a dream come true. Chip asked near my ear, "Are you going to the winter dance already? Do you have a date?"

The tears came on unexpectedly, bubbling up from inside my chest. Chip leaned back and looked at me. "Whoa. Hey. What's wrong?" His eyes were sincere, his cheeks remarkably pink below that halo of blond hair.

"Nothing. I don't know."

"What'd I say? Laura?" When he lifted a finger to wipe my face, I stopped him.

"No, don't. I'm just . . . I'm sorry, I can't. I'm sorry."

I pulled away, and as I ran out of the gym I heard the other girls whispering behind my back, "What happened? What's wrong with her?"

. . .

Well. You can probably guess what the problem was.

As much as I loved Tim, I had only seen him once in the last two years—in high school time, that was like one day out of twenty years. And the four semesters I'd been at SHA, I had to admit, had changed me, just like my parents had hoped. It's the good and bad of education: as the world grows bigger the more you learn about it, so the neighborhood you came from seems to grow smaller. Now all of Tim's talk about shopping for homes and settling down began to make me nervous. I was only seventeen years old, after all, still just a girl. Maybe in Zachary, Tim's plans wouldn't have seemed out of place, but here at SHA none of my classmates got married and had babies right after they graduated. They went to college, got jobs, dated, had fun. What was his hurry, after all?

And the truth was, most of our relationship had been through letters, hadn't it? Letters that, in spite of all their sweet words, had an air of make-believe precisely because they were only words on paper. They were abstractions, barely real. If a letter got lost in the mail, the world inside its envelope might as well have never existed. Or if you left a letter in the rain, the ink would blur and wash right off, carrying with it any evidence of the reality the words had ever represented.

But all this was mere justification, I knew, for the troubling realization that as my life at Sacred Heart Academy began to feel brighter and more hopeful, the life of Tim's letters began to feel that much more dim and complicated. It was the giddy teenage world of Winter Formals with aluminum foil stars and dream dates, pitted against the frighteningly adult world of tours of duty in Vietnam and down payments on aluminum-sided homes on muddy suburban lots in small-town Zachary.

And honestly, which do you think a seventeen-year-old girl would choose? Which would you choose, Liz?

The choice became all the more difficult when around this same time, Tim's letters began to undergo a change. I barely registered it at first. Tim was such a naturally optimistic person that it would have been hard to recognize anything like despair creeping into his words. And the story only appeared in bits and pieces, never all at once—just a fragment here, a sidelong reference there. But as the weeks went on, it became apparent that something awful had happened to Tim, something that cut a deep and lasting scar on his soul.

The story, as I was able to piece it together, turned around an incident that happened when he and his buddy were out on a surveillance mission. By his accounts, everything was done by the book. For three or four weeks they had been monitoring suspicious activity in a village in a neighboring valley. There were trucks rolling in and out of the village at night, fluctuations in the population, new huts being erected around the perimeter. Radio transmissions eventually confirmed that the village was a transport hub for the Viet Cong.

So one morning after getting the go-ahead, Tim called in the coordinates for an air strike. Twenty minutes later a single F-4 Phantom jet screamed over their heads and dropped a neat load of ordnance: two missilelike Hammer bombs that tore straight through the palm trees toward the village, followed by one stumpy-looking napalm canister that tumbled end over end as it fell, like something accidentally dropped from the back of the plane. Explosions rumbled like thunder up from the valley floor. The jet veered off to the left and disappeared over the hills, leaving clouds of dense black smoke and fire pluming in the valley. An eerie quiet settled on the mountaintop. All the birds had fallen silent. Mission accomplished.

This was when Tim and his buddy usually packed up their gear and headed back to base. But, oddly, radio transmissions continued to issue from the bombed village. Since they were the only troops in the vicinity, Tim and his partner were ordered in to "have a look-see."

"I normally have nothing to do with this kind of thing, you understand," Tim explained in one of the letters. "We do our radio business and get out of there." But orders were orders. They hiked down from their camp on the ridge, helmets on, rifles out, just two skinny radio geeks in boots and camouflage clomping and slipping down the mountainside. They came out onto the dirt road leading to the village. Black smoke continued to billow over the palm trees ahead, a good sign that they'd hit a weapons cache.

The first thing was the sound, Tim wrote. They heard it as they approached the village, a high, spooky wail, something stuck halfway between animal and human. And then the smell—a smell that Tim had never encountered before, but one that his body instinctively recognized and recoiled from, causing him to buckle and vomit, right there on the trail.

. . .

That was as far as Tim ever got in the story in his letters to me that year. But over the weeks he kept coming back again and again to those same details: how he was just doing his job, calling in the coordinates; the eerie silence on the mountaintop after the jet dropped its load; then he and his buddy hiking down the hill and seeing the black smoke above the trees. And at last, that strange keening noise, followed by the gut-wrenching smell as they entered the village . . .

Well. I had seen only snippets of the war on TV, but even in those brief color-washed flashes there were horrors enough to haunt a lifetime. So I had an idea of what Tim had seen but could not tell. The wonder of it was that he had been spared for so long. Because what Tim had seen at last when they entered the village that day, I knew, was only the manifest consequence of his radio work, numbered coordinates revealed as flesh-and-blood people.

What he had finally seen was the truth of war, which is death: fathers and sons, mothers and daughters, slaughtered.

IX

So you're officially a missing person now, Liz. For what that's worth.

We found a sympathetic night desk officer at the police station who agreed to register the case. He went through a checklist with us over the phone. Had we contacted our child's friends and classmates? Had we informed relatives? Had we spoken to neighbors? Had we visited places we knew our child to frequent? Yes yes yes yes. Your father even thought to look for clues on your computer—correspondence, Web searches, whatever—but he couldn't get past the log-in without your password. He's gone to the police station now to sign the forms and leave a photograph.

Your photograph: we had kind of a fight over that. It's because of the stress, I know. I found a lovely snapshot from your junior high school graduation. You remember that nice blue dress we bought with the white belt and matching collar? You looked so pretty in that. In the picture you're holding your diploma with a bouquet of flowers, the sun full on your face, smiling. Your father, though, thought we should use a more recent photo and found one on the bulletin board in your room. I suppose it was taken by one of your friends. You're wearing camouflage pants and a too-small black T-shirt, with your black eyeliner and black lipstick and brow ring, and holding what looks like a plastic beer cup in one hand. "But this is her. This is how she looks," your father said. I'm the one who always insists on telling it like it is, he said, looking the truth square in the face and all that, but when it comes to my own daughter, it's like I'm wearing blinders. He may be right, I don't know. In the end, he took the ugly photo.

One thing at least your father and I agree on is that you've changed, Liz. That I can see plainly enough. You used to be so cheerful. Your girlfriends would come over and you all would laugh yourselves silly trying on clothes or making up cookie recipes in the kitchen. You dressed nicely then. You smiled for photographs, and talked to us over dinner, and looked forward to summer vacations. And then suddenly it seemed it was all over. You began locking your bedroom door, and skipping meals, and generally keeping so much to yourself that now you're little more than a dark shadow flying through the den and out the door to jump into the cars of mysterious strangers we've never met. When we ask where you're going, you say, "Out." With whom? "Friends." And you'll be back . . . ? "Later."

We've wondered, you know, your father and I, if it's drugs. Ever since the infamous lake house incident with Missy and friends last summer when the whole gang of you were dragged to the Pointe Coupee Parish police station, it's only natural that we would become suspicious. Your father, however, who claims some knowledge in this area, says you don't exhibit any of the usual signs of drug abuse: you seem healthy enough, your eyes aren't glazed, and your speech, when you speak, is coherent at least. Your father's been wrong before, of course, but this time I sincerely hope he's not.

Now the house is really quiet. There's just the hum of the refrigerator in the kitchen and the low buzz of crickets coming from the yard. Other than that, the rooms stand silent, like they've been abandoned. A home shouldn't be this quiet, Liz. This much quiet is unsettling; it leaves too much room for memory and imagination, for fear and dread. Every time another car rounds the corner I jerk up, thinking it might be you.

X

Wartime or not, high school goes on.

I didn't go with Chip to the winter dance that year. But he didn't give up, and by the end of the second semester I agreed to go to his senior prom with him. My friends said I was lucky he even asked me after I'd been so weird to him. And what was the big deal, anyway? It was only a dance, after all. What harm could there be in a little school prom?

Soo Chee borrowed a dress from her older sister for me. A tight, pink silk tube, it wasn't like the dresses other SHA girls picked out at Godchaux's, but it was sleek and flattering in an Oriental kind of way. The high-heeled shoes I got from Christy Lee, the beaded handbag from Anne Harding. The afternoon of the dance, they all came over to my room to help me get ready.

"He'll have whiskey and try to get you drunk," Christy Lee warned, working on my hair. "Don't let him."

"And don't eat too much at dinner, no matter how good the food is," said Soo Chee, fussing over my dress. Her mother worked as a seamstress, so Soo Chee knew how to take up the hem. "Don't forget your toothbrush. You keep it in your handbag with your makeup. Take a handkerchief, too, so you can wipe your hands when they get sweaty. Boys hate sweaty hands."

"Should I bring money?"

"God no. You're the date," said Anne. "You're like the princess for the evening. Don't pay for anything."

"Make him grovel," said Christy. "Make him beg."

My roommate, Melissa, watched from the side of the room, fascinated. "Have you seriously never been on a date before?"

After they finished, my friends stood back to admire their handiwork. Soo Chee adjusted the dress so it fell properly. "Now you look good."

"Stand up straight," Anne said. "Don't slouch."

Christy took photos of us all, Anne cried a little, and I promised to tell them everything that happened that night. When word came that Chip had arrived and was waiting outside, my friends followed me down for more pictures. Sister Hagatha-Agatha watched us suspiciously from the door of the convent building. The school had waived the usual curfew for boarding students attending the prom, and even though a whole slew of teachers and parents would be on hand to chaperone the dance, Hagatha-Agatha made it plain she didn't approve of this much liberty for young Catholic ladies. Chip good-naturedly made a show out of pinning on my corsage, then offering me his arm, then holding open the door of his car for me. Before climbing into the driver's seat, he called out, "Don't worry, Sister. I won't let her take advantage of me!"—daring to do what none of us girls ever did, which was to try to joke with Sister Agatha. He honked the horn, and as we drove off waving goodbye from the windows I felt, if only for a moment, like we really were royalty.

. . .

Do boys and girls your age go out on dates like this anymore, Liz? I've only heard you talk about hanging out and hooking up, which doesn't sound much like what Chip and I did that evening. But who knows. Maybe the difference is only in the details. Maybe when you hang out and hook up you feel the same nervous excitement that I felt then, seventeen years old and on my first real date.

Chip had made dinner reservations for us at the Riverside Hotel downtown, the one that used to have the revolving restaurant at the top. We headed straight there in his ship of a car. It was his father's car, actually, but I could see that Chip had taken pains to get it ready for us. He had washed and polished it, inside and out, and sprayed it with pine-scented air freshener. On the transmission hump between our legs sat a small caddy holding a fresh miniature box of Kleenex and two new rolls of peppermint Life Savers. He worried over the radio and air-conditioner controls. "That's not too cold on you, is it?"

The Cadillac Sedan DeVille was different from the Coupe DeVille in that it had four doors instead of two, he explained when I asked. His mom hated two doors, so that's why they always got four doors. I nodded and expressed interest in whatever he said and kept asking questions, as I'd been coached by my girlfriends. "And this car was made when, exactly?" I asked, and, "What other lines of cars are you fond of?" We went on like this for ten or fifteen minutes until Chip, exasperated, said, "Oh for Christ's sake, can we forget about the car? Who gives a damn about the car anyway?" I laughed and felt the weight fly off my chest, and knew that we'd do just fine that evening.

The maitre d' at the restaurant was Chip's cousin, so we not only got a table by the window, we got wine with our dinner, too. I tried to act nonchalant about the wine, the candles, the beautiful china and silverware, and the shockingly high prices on the menu, but it was the nicest restaurant I'd ever been to in my life. My parents had never brought me to a place like this before. I ordered the sirloin strip because Chip ordered the sirloin strip, and the Caesar salad because he ordered the Caesar salad. "No, no, I like that, too," I insisted.

Over dinner, Chip told me about his acceptance at Tulane University in New Orleans for the fall. He wasn't sure yet if he would major in business or premed, he said, but he figured he had a semester or two to decide. He'd live on campus his freshman year since that was easiest, and then probably move into a frat house his sophomore year. Some of his buddies were talking about pledging Phi Kappa Alpha, but Chip's father had been a Kappa Sig, so there was a good chance he'd end up there, too. He might've been talking about studying in Paris at the Sorbonne, it sounded so elite to me.

"God, that's just so . . ." I said.

"What?"

"I mean, in Zachary hardly anyone goes to college. If a boy's very ambitious, he might go to ag school at LSU. But then he'd drop out after the first semester because what's the use in learning all that chemistry when everything you need to know about farming you can learn from your daddy?"

Chip chuckled.

"And if you're a girl, well, forget it. Your choice is basically to get married or not."

"And if you're a girl named Laura Jenkins?"

"If you're a girl named Laura Jenkins . . ."

"Yeah. What're her plans?"

From the window of the revolving restaurant I watched the state capitol drift by over Chip's right shoulder, followed by the gas jets of the oil refineries lighting up the night sky like Roman candles. Down below, the shiny black river caught the reflected glare of the fires as it streamed past Baton Rouge, on down toward New Orleans and points farther south, where the waters spilled into the Gulf of Mexico to merge at last with the great wide ocean beyond. As we floated high above it all at our white-draped table, the world seemed to open itself up like a gilt-edged invitation to a life full of promise and glamour.

Chip watched me from across the table. "Some deep thoughts going on there."

"Not so deep."

"What is it, then?"

I twisted the stem of the wineglass in my fingers. Why shouldn't we talk about this? We were adults, after all, having an adult conversation over a steak dinner in this very sophisticated restaurant. And Chip looked so handsome in his rented tuxedo, and his expression was so earnest and open.

"Well," I said. "If you must know. There's this boy."

"Oh."

"I mean, a friend, he's a good friend. He's in Vietnam now. I met him two, almost three years ago, in Zachary. Before I came here. We kind of, you know, we dated. But then I got sent to Sacred Heart and he enlisted."

"Wow. I didn't realize. . . . How old is he?"

"Um, twenty."

"And you're . . . He's your boyfriend?"

"I don't know. Yes. I mean . . . he was my first. You have to understand. I was fifteen years old, he was a senior. I had never met a boy like Tim before." I explained how we got to know each other, how my parents hated him, how Tim's letters practically saved my life during my first year at Sacred Heart. And how, just as I needed him then, he needed me now while he was in Vietnam.

I looked up at Chip. "He wants us to get married when he comes home."

"Gosh. Wow."

"Yeah."

Chip took a big gulp of his wine. "I didn't know any of this."

"I know."

"When's he coming back?"

"He reenlisted. He's got about six more months."

"And then?"

"And then . . ."

"And then you'll get married?"

"I don't know. I don't know, Chip. I'm not even a senior yet. How can I get married? But Tim wants to. He says it's all he thinks about now. He's saving his money to buy us a house in Zachary."

"Jesus, Laura."

"I shouldn't have told you."

"No, I'm glad you did. I'm glad."

He frowned as he grabbed a dinner roll and began buttering it. He didn't look glad. I sipped water, and as the restaurant took us on another tour of Baton Rouge I waited to see who would speak next. I was afraid I'd ruined our evening by introducing Tim. It was like I'd summoned him right into the restaurant, and now he was standing by our table in his muddy combat boots, his rifle slung on his back, staring down on our dinner looking hurt and betrayed. I couldn't pretend he didn't exist. But what was I going to do? Tell him "We're having dinner. Go away, please. Leave us alone. Go back to your war"?

Later, after Chip had paid for our meal and pulled out my chair and was leading us through the elegant old lobby of the hotel, I linked my hand in his arm.

"I'm sorry."

"Don't be."

"No. Really."

"I just want us to have a good time tonight," he said, rubbing his toe on the pavement as we waited for the valet to bring the car.

I gave his arm a squeeze. "Don't worry, we will. I promise."

. . .

Remember what I said about you learning from my mistakes? About how the whole moral purpose of this story is to help you lead a better life than I did? Well. Keep that in mind.

My friend Christy was right. Chip had brought whiskey for the evening, a neat flask of Jack Daniel's tucked in the glove compartment of his father's car. When we arrived at the Hilton hotel, Chip stopped the car in a dark corner of the parking lot and took out the bottle. On the first sip the whiskey seared the inside of my throat. "You'll want to go easy on that," he said. "Just a taste on the lips."

"I'm fine," I said, coughing.

We listened to the radio as we passed the bottle. Chip began to tell me about a horse he once had. They used to keep him at the family farm—a farm that I gathered wasn't like the farm I grew up on, but more like a summer home. The horse's name was Geronimo, an American paint. Chip took good care of him, and the horse understood that he belonged to Chip and would become snappish whenever someone else tried to ride him. He was like Chip's best friend all through junior high, until he got a brain disease that made his muscles go slack. At first he stumbled around like he was drunk, but then it got so bad that he couldn't stand up and they had to shoot him. "Not me. I didn't shoot him," Chip said. He couldn't bring himself to do it. His father had to do it.

Chip stopped talking and we sat a moment in silence.

"Gosh. That's terrible," I said. "I'm so sorry to hear that."

"It was a long time ago," Chip said, and abruptly leaned forward to adjust the radio dial. "I don't even know why I told you that. It's not even a funny story."

But his story, I felt, with its hint of loss and love, bound us together in some deeper way, adding an extra intimacy to the evening. It was this feeling, I believe, that would encourage me to do what I did later.

"You ready?" Chip said. "Let's go."

The theme of the CHS 1972 senior prom was "Nights in White Satin," named after a ponderous Moody Blues song popular that year. Everything was draped in white satiny cloth, naturally, and a whole gang of boys had come dressed in matching white tuxedos, calling themselves the Knights in White Satin. We shared a table with Chip's friends and their dates, some of whom I knew from Sacred Heart. No charity cases here, only teenagers dressed up in tuxedos and gowns, their shoes shiny, their hair shiny, a little bit tipsy, celebrating all their good fortune—fortune that came so easily and was so common here as to be all but unnoticed.

Some songs popular that year, in case you're curious: "American Pie," "Alone Again, Naturally," "Lean on Me," "I Can See Clearly Now," and "Bang a Gong (Get It On)." We danced the shake, the hitchhike, and the otherwise general kind of flopping around we did in those days, working up a sweat that mingled with the smell of hairspray and deodorant to create a sweet, heady stew of teenage exuberance. Dropping back down in our chairs, we swallowed cups of Coke that had been spiked with rum under the table. When someone brought out a camera for photos, Chip threw his arm around me. A girl at the table remarked on what an attractive couple we made.

"Yeah, too bad she's already taken," Chip said.

"What? Who is it?" the girl asked.

"An older man. Major in the army," Chip said.

"Not a major," I said.

"I like soldiers," another girl said.

"They're gonna get married when he comes home."

"Chip—" I said.

"Is that true?"

"Little home there in Zachary. Couple of broken cars in the front yard. Kids rolling around in the dirt."

"Chip—"

"Are we invited to the wedding?"

"No," Chip said.

"Yes. Of course. Why not?" I said. "You're all invited. Please come." Then I added, just to be funny, "Bring your own beer. We'll decorate the trailer, get some balloons and crepe paper."

Everyone at the table laughed.

"Zachary. Yuck," a girl said. "You'll be barefoot and pregnant before you're twenty."

"That's me. Trailer bride," I said, sipping my rum and Coke through a straw. "I can hardly wait."

"How many kids?"

"Two. No, five," I said.

"Make it seven," another girl said. "One for each day of the week."

"You can name them that way," a boy said. " 'Monday, come over here! Leave Wednesday alone.' "

"We'll grow snap beans up the side of the trailer," I said, on a roll now. "I'll plant petunias in old tractor tires."

"Laura Loo! Get on here and snap those beans," Chip said in a funny Cajun voice. "I want my okra. Now!" He hugged my shoulders. "Look, honey, I done shot a coon for the gumbo. Mm-mm good."

"Gumbo. Yee haw!" a boy cried.

"Save the fur, honey!" I said. "I'll make pants for little Thursday. He done worn his out rolling in the mud."

This won me an even bigger laugh. Drunk and inspired, brilliant in our gowns and tuxedos, we went on making fun of poor Cajuns like Tim until the band started playing "Nights in White Satin" and we were obliged to dance.

"Come on, Laura Loo," said Chip, taking my hand to lead me to the floor. "We gotta go fais do-do."

. . .

Four o'clock in the morning. See us lounging in a suburban rec room, pale-faced and bleary-eyed in our striped bell-bottom pants and denim vests. We'd done the postprom parties, the postprom party breakfasts, and now the girls' hairdos had all gone flat, and the boys' faces, slick with sweat and oil, had sprouted tiny whiteheads, budding up overnight like mushrooms after a storm. As Elton John played softly from a cheap stereo in the next room, boys began rummaging for their car keys and rousing their dates from sofas. Someone was busy cleaning up vomit in the bathroom. Someone else's parents were calling on the phone, wondering where they were. Stumbling across dewy purple lawns, we shouted drunkenly affectionate goodbyes to one another; and even though we knew we'd all be seeing each other at school later that week, there was a rush of sentimentality as we threw our arms around each other and said how this night was the best of them all, we would never forget it, we would be friends forever, friends for life.

I leaned against Chip in the Cadillac Sedan DeVille, my arm hooked into his, as he piloted us slowly through town. The streetlights were still on, casting their watery glow across the flat yards and empty parking lots of Baton Rouge. Tired, happy, I was floating on that dreamy euphoria that comes from just the right blend of sleeplessness, alcohol, caffeine, and youth. You must have tasted it yourself by now, Liz, though you might not recognize it yet as something rare and special, and therefore to be handled with special caution.

At a park overlooking the LSU lake, Chip turned in and stopped the car. We talked a bit, snuggling up against each other. His button-down shirt felt dry-cleaner pressed, and his after-prom loafers held a deep burgundy shine. He smelled nice. Clean. Secure.

He pointed out his home across the lake. Following his finger, I could make out, framed by two enormous live oaks on the opposite shore, a white columned porch and a red-brick chimney. The lake was still and black, and the moon, sunk low behind us, laid a milky white path across the water. I had the fantastic notion that Chip and I could step from the car and walk hand in hand across that white road to his house and up the porch steps to the front door and keep walking forever into a rich, easy future. It would be that simple. Life would be that simple.

How do I justify what I did next? It would be easy enough to blame the alcohol, but there was more to it than that. There was genuine affection involved. I knew that Chip was graduating soon and going to Tulane. This was possibly our last chance to be alone together before he left. Certainly this was the only senior prom he would ever attend, and the only night after a senior prom he would ever know. And he was so kind and polite and decent. I thought of it as a gift I might offer him. "I want this night to be special for you," I said, and meant it as sincerely as I had ever meant anything.

"My god," he whispered. "What are you doing?"

"Shh—" I said.

"Laura—"

"Do you like that?" I found his right hand on the seat and held it in my left. He squeezed my fingers. I only wanted to make him happy. The radio dial cast a blue-green glow into the front seat, as if we were sinking underwater. Sounds became muted and distant, and all of our movements seemed to be in slow motion. His brass belt buckle glinted in the submarine light. The song on the radio, I remember, was "Close to You" by the Carpenters.

"Is that okay? Do you like that? Do you?"

"Oh my god," he said, miles above me. "Oh dear god, yes."

. . .

In case you're counting, Liz, that was the third time I betrayed Tim that evening. In the days that followed the prom, it wasn't the act itself, no matter how stupidly inappropriate it might have been, that caused me such remorse. Rather, it was how easily I had disowned Tim that racked me with guilt, making me feel lower than Judas, the lowest, most untrustworthy friend in the world. And as the weeks went on and Chip became more and more peculiar and unresponsive and eventually stopped talking to me altogether, I felt it was only fitting retribution for my unfaithfulness that he should turn away from me.

I don't blame Chip. He was and always would be a kind and decent Catholic boy—that would never change about him. But as a kind and decent Catholic boy, he also had certain expectations about girls, and in particular the type of girl he might bring home to his parents one day, the type he might safely marry knowing that she was as pure and untested as his own mother had been on the day of her wedding. I, clearly, was not that girl. And it was only just, I felt, that in addition to the private guilt I suffered for my betrayal of Tim, I also suffered the public shame of soon being branded by my peers and classmates at Cathedral High School and Sacred Heart Academy as a low-class, easy slut.

XI

Your father's out mowing the grass again. It's eight o'clock at night and he's mowing the grass. The noise of the engine builds to a roar as he pushes it past the rear of the house, fades to a whine as he steers it to a dark corner of the yard.

Do you remember when you were three years old and caught pneumonia? You probably don't. Your father took off work for a week so he could sit by your bedside and rub you with witch hazel and feed you chicken broth. He loves you, he does, he just doesn't know how to show it anymore. As best as I can explain it, Liz, that's why he's out there now mowing the grass, the grass he's already mowed.

Before going out your father suggested I take a break. Why was I still obsessively writing this letter? Wasn't I tired? What was the point? I told him I need to finish before you get home. He looked at me oddly, started to say something, but then left. I didn't ask what he meant to say; I don't need to know. The writing gives me comfort. Isn't that enough? This, I tell myself, is at least one thing I can do now to make up for whatever wrongs I've done.

Because the question that still haunts me most, daughter, is why? Why did you run? Has your life here been that unbearable? Did that one slap sting that much? Or is it something else, something that troubles you more than I'll ever imagine? Because I know, you see, how much a daughter can hide from a mother. I've heard you crying behind your bedroom door, and I've hated myself for not having compassion enough even to knock, telling myself that your problems are your own making, and that the best thing I can do for you is to let you live and learn, that I should respect your privacy like you demand I should. . . . I've listened, and I've walked away until I couldn't hear you crying anymore. That, Liz, is why I keep writing this letter.

Here comes the mower again, back around behind the house. My hand's tired, my energy is flagging, and I'm not especially looking forward to this next part. But there are things you still don't know yet, and I promised I would tell everything.

XII

No doubt you've heard about the sexual revolution of my generation—women's liberation, the pill, ban the bra, all that. How I wish I'd been a part of it. But at Sacred Heart Academy we may as well have been living in the nineteenth century. Our sexual education, what little there was of it, was all tangled up with our religious education. It was a forced, unhappy marriage.

Sister Hagatha-Agatha taught both "Church History and Doctrine" and "Health and Our Bodies." Being old, she often confounded the two, but this hardly mattered, since she preached the same lessons no matter what the class. We learned the difference between purgatory and limbo, and what is a venial sin and what is a mortal sin, and what are the respective punishments for these two categories of sin. She taught us the nine orders of angels and brought in pictures of each type so that, presumably, we would know who we were talking to if we ever got to heaven.

On rainy days, in an odd, low pious voice that bordered on the creepy, Hagatha-Agatha told us stories of all the most exotic saints and gruesome martyrs. I'm sure no student of hers will ever forget Saint Catherine of Siena,

Virgin—she who consecrated her virginity to God while still a child, and later, to escape marriage, cut off all her hair, "beautiful golden-brown hair that reached down to her waist," Hagatha-Agatha told us. "Cut it all off!" Thereafter, for her entire adult life she scourged herself three times daily with chains, and wore an iron-spiked girdle underneath her smock. ("Just try to imagine that, girls. Sharp spikes, sharp like needles, piercing the skin above your ribs. Every time you breathe they dig deeper.") Saint Catherine of Siena, Virgin, lived only on boiled herbs and water, and fasted from Ash Wednesday until Ascension Day, accepting as her only sustenance for the entire forty days nothing but the blessed Eucharist. She humbly served the poor and afflicted, and once (Why, oh why, did you have to tell us this, Sister Agatha?) drank cupfuls of cancerous puss from a sick old woman whose only thank-you was to hurl more vile abuse at the saint. In a vision near the end of her life, God presented Catherine with two crowns, one of gold and the other of thorns, and ordered her to choose. Saint Catherine of Siena, Virgin, answered that her only solace was in pain and suffering, and eagerly seized the crown of thorns and pressed it upon her head.

This, Liz, was the tenor of our sexual-religious education at Sacred Heart. Little surprise that girls came away feeling mighty confused, if not outright repulsed, by sex. I think it also helps to explain what happened when I returned to Sacred Heart for my senior year.

With no one to confide in at home, I suffered miserably all summer over my abandonment by Chip Benton, and now he had gone, left for college in New Orleans without even returning my phone calls. Back at school the first week, I made the mistake of spilling my heart out to my roommate,

Melissa. It was during one of those late-night orgies of conversational intimacy that an all-girls' school encourages, and I said much more than I should have. She swore not to tell anyone about me and Chip, but by the week's end I began to notice a subtle but distinct change in those around me. I heard whispers behind my back, and underclassmen stared at me oddly in the bathroom. I don't think I was imagining these things, not entirely; someone even took the trouble to scratch "J = Jenkins = Jezebel" on the front of my locker. My guilty conscience only fueled my suspicions, until, walking down the corridor, I felt as if there was a red letter *J* emblazoned on the front of my uniform. *Look,* this letter announced to all who passed, *here is the Jezebel Laura Jenkins from Zachary who cheated on her boyfriend in Vietnam by committing obscene acts with her prom date in his car*. I hugged my books to my chest and tried to keep my head up high like Hester Prynne, but oh, it was hard. Instead, I withdrew more from the society of the school, and the more I withdrew, the more I felt ostracized, until I was that fifteen-year-old transfer student again, sobbing into her pillow at night. What should have been my happiest, brightest year was already turning into a disaster. This, I thought, only proved how conditional my standing was at the school. As easily as my classmates' favor had been granted to me, it could as easily be snatched away. They would never let me forget that I was only an ill-bred farm girl who never really belonged among the Baton Rouge debutantes at SHA. Once a charity case . . .

Sister Mary Margaret noticed my unhappiness. The good nun tried to speak to me once or twice in the library, but there was no way I could begin to unpack the whole sordid story for her, and so I didn't even try.

"It's nothing, Sister," I told her.

"Are you sure?"

"I'm fine."

"Well . . . if you ever need to talk." She nodded significantly toward the bookshelves. "Have you seen? Elizabeth Barrett Browning?" Sister M&M was still acting as a secret letter carrier for Tim and me. Every week or two, a new one would faithfully arrive, transported from the jungles of Vietnam by some incredible series of conveyance (army jeep—helicopter—carrier plane—truck—mailman—Sister M&M) to miraculously appear tucked between the yellowing pages of a neglected book here in our small library at SHA. I mustered a smile. "I will. Thank you. Thank you, Sister."

Tim's letters, though, when they arrived, brought me little comfort that semester. The poor boy was still mired in regret over the bombing raid he'd called down months ago on that Vietnamese village.

He'd tried everything to forget, he wrote. "I'd be ashamed to tell you what all I've tried. But I guess it's no more than what most boys over here do." Nothing helped. Night after night, it didn't matter what bar or hovel he was in, he'd find himself hiking again into that wasted village. The smoke pluming above the palms, his buddy's water canteen clicking against his ammo belt. And then—there was nothing to stop it from coming back—the high, agonized wail as they approached the first house, followed by the gut-wrenching smell of burning flesh. "You understand I had no choice in this," he repeated. "I was just doing my job." He seemed to be sinking into a depression far worse than mine. And then midsemester, something happened that brought him even deeper.

One day after watch duty he was lounging in his hut when he saw a spider crawling up the wall. It was a giant hairy red and black thing, almost the size of his hand. At the camp they called them jumping spiders, or cave spiders, or just "big hairy gook spiders."

He picked up his pistol from the side of the bed, aimed, and shot the thing, blasting a nice hole in the corner of his hut. The cleaning boy, a Vietnamese kid they called Bo, came running, saw what was left of the spider, and freaked out. When the boy turned to Tim, the expression on his face was like he was seeing a ghost. "What? What is it?" Tim asked. Bo wouldn't answer, only began rapidly mumbling prayers to himself. Tim grabbed his arm, but the kid jerked free and ran out of the hut.

Tim asked around after this, and apparently killing a spider was about the unluckiest thing a person could do in Vietnam. "It's crazy, I know," he wrote. "I don't buy any of that stuff. What does a spider have to with whether or not Charlie gets a crack at me?" But the cleaning boy began to avoid him, running to the opposite side of the road, even ducking around corners when he saw Tim coming. It made him feel, Tim wrote, like he wore the mark of death on him.

His letters began to take on a darkly philosophical tone. He wrote about things he'd never mentioned before, friends of his who had gone out on routine patrols, or even just down the street to buy farm eggs in the next village, and had never come back. He wrote about the superstitions that soldiers came up with to explain away the randomness of life and death. How you should never say aloud the number of days you had left, for instance—that was sure to kill you. Or how some claimed that they could tell how long a newbie would last the minute he stepped off the chopper; it was a gutted look behind the eyes, or a hesitant gait that gave it away. "That one's a goner," they'd say. "Two months, tops." But as far as Tim could see, death didn't play by any rules. A clumsy blueleg from Minnesota who could barely load a rifle would go home without a scratch, while the smartest, sleekest tracker you ever met would get blown to a gory paste his third day out. Didn't have anything to do with how good or bad a person was, neither. Line them all up—the nun, the priest, the shopkeeper, the rapist, the murdering NVA, the screaming teenage girl in a straw hat holding a live baby boy, the smoke still rising from its black charred body: you think there was any difference between them? There wasn't no difference. Didn't matter who you were or what you did, we all came to the same dead end. "And if you can figure that one out, I'll be happy to hear it," Tim wrote.

But even as his letters dipped into this darkest of places, he still clung to one desperate hope, and that was me.

"I picture you running up to meet me when I step off the bus in Zachary at Christmastime," he wrote. "You look just like I left you, only better. You're wearing shorts. (I always picture you wearing shorts even if it's the middle of winter, hope you don't mind.) I pick you up and hug you and kiss you and nobody can say nothing because I just came back from Vietnam and I got a whole mess of medals on my chest." We'd have a little house there near the woods, nothing but peace and quiet, and for about a year he wouldn't do anything but sit and look at me and we'd make love all day.

"My good luck charm," he wrote. "Laura. All I got to do is

turn my arm up to see you. That's permanent, won't ever go away."

. . .

Elizabeth, see if you can understand this. I stopped reading his letters. I couldn't bear to hear any more about his ugly war. Why did he have to tell me all that? What could I do to help him? I had my own problems to worry about. I couldn't take on the burden of being his lifesaver, too, his one and only hope.

The first one I removed from Elizabeth Barrett Browning and didn't open right away because I knew how depressing it would be; then I didn't open it for the rest of the day, and then a week had passed and it was still in the drawer of my desk, unopened, beside the scrapbook I'd abandoned long ago. And then the next letter came, and I put it in the drawer with the first. Then another one. Later, I told myself. I would read them later, when I was stronger. But by semester's end I had a small stack, light as the airmail paper they were written on but weighted with the accumulated guilt of my avoidance.

He was killed, they said, in his sleep. Two weeks before his discharge, three clumsy mortar shells were lobbed from a hill where they hadn't seen any North Vietnamese for a year and a half. One landed just short of the base fence, one landed on the wash shed of the kitchen, and one landed on a hut that wasn't even Tim's but had an air conditioner and the fellow was away and so Tim was using it. Even the army morticians, with all their glue and stuffing and wax, couldn't make him resemble a human being. His remains were delivered to Zachary in a closed coffin draped with an American flag, which was how he was displayed on the altar of St. Aloysius Catholic Church that chilly winter day between Christmas and New Year 1973.

Holiday decorations were still up, evergreen wreaths on the walls, a nativity scene at the front of the church. I recognized some of Tim's old high school buddies and a few of his relatives who'd driven in from Lafayette. I wondered how Jack would get through it, remembering his wife lying in the same spot on the same altar four years ago. "First Suzy and now this," people whispered. "Good Lord."

Unlike the first, this service was a stark, brief affair with no flowers, no incense, no organist. The lights of the church hadn't even been turned on, as I recall, and the only illumination was a watery glow of red, blue, and yellow seeping through the stained-glass windows and spilling across the wooden pews and floors that damp gray afternoon. I sat next to Jack in the front row because he asked me to. We barely spoke, and when we did it was mostly to exchange factual and necessary information: go here, do this, give that lady a hand, would you. Jack didn't allow a sermon from the priest, just the minimum required words to send the soul to heaven. In a moment of terrible insight during the prayers and sniffling, I recognized this service to be the exact opposite of the service that Tim had always dreamed of for his homecoming: sorrow instead of joy, an end instead of a beginning, and one instead of two at the altar.

Soon we were lining up to pay our respects. Nearing the coffin, I tried to picture Tim's soul rising to heaven. His body would be smooth and pure as I remembered it, but transparent. The ghost-soul of Tim would be met in the sky by Saint Michael, who would escort him up past the clouds, through dark space and stars, bypassing purgatory to ascend swiftly into the radiant sphere of heaven, where, the nuns assured us, the blessed lived in supreme happiness in the presence of God forever and ever.

But as I touched my lips to the dark wood of the casket, I couldn't hold on to this vision. I was conscious only of the unnatural gloss of the wood, and of the creak of the floorboards behind me, and of the priest standing to one side coughing and rustling his vestments. He might have been a man waiting at a service station to have a tire changed. There was nothing sacred there that day. What I mean to say is, as far as I was concerned, God has vanished, flown far away, leaving us poor human beings with nothing more than pieces of charred bone and flesh in a wooden box. That's all it was.

At the cemetery, Jack stood back blinking as the coffin was settled in the dirt in front of his wife's marble memorial. He seemed not to know what to do with his hands—to let them hang at his sides, or put them in his pockets, or fold them below his waist as the priest was doing. The clouds of his breath huffed in front of his gray face. He looked all of a sudden like a brittle, lost old man, and if I felt anything at all that day, it was a soft, vague pity for Jack. The undertaker was standing by with the shovel, and Jack obligingly took it in hand to toss the first clod of dirt into the hole. It landed with a flop on top of the coffin, and Jack passed back the shovel. A black crow cawed impatiently from the branch of a nearby pine, telling us to hurry up and get it over with.

I hadn't expected to accompany Jack back to his trailer that evening, but after all the friends had left and the relatives had gone back to Lafayette, there was no one left to care for him but me. The trailer was cluttered and cheerless, even smaller than I remembered it. I cooked dinner for him and tried to put things in order. The flowers he didn't want. The trifolded American flag I set to one side on the kitchen table. I felt bad leaving him for the night. I didn't see how he could stand to stay out there in the woods in that cold aluminum cave all by himself.

"Sure you'll be all right?"

"I managed for two and a half years. I reckon I can manage the rest," he said from the doorway.

For the remainder of the holiday, I ended up going to sit with him for a few hours every evening. After I cooked dinner for him, we would do jigsaw puzzles at the fold-down table. We didn't talk much, not at first, but it didn't feel as if we had to. It was okay just to be there. At the time I thought I was doing this as a favor to Jack, but I came to understand that I needed these visits as much as he did. There was no crying, no dramatics, and when we spoke of Tim it was in the familiar, fond way that you might speak of an old classmate you hadn't seen for a while. We just were getting through it the best we could, I suppose, providing each other with the simple, undemanding presence of another person.

My parents, for their part, didn't dare to protest my nightly visits. They sensed they didn't have any say in the matter, even as I took food from my mother's kitchen and carried it to Jack's in my father's car. At certain times in a person's life, I believe, their will takes over their actions, making them as driven and unalterable as the weather. My parents could no sooner have stopped me from going than they could have stopped the rain. And anyway, what were they going to protest? The boy they hated had been blown to bits. They should've been overjoyed.

I visited Jack once more on the day I was due to go back to Sacred Heart. I made biscuits for breakfast, we had coffee, and before I left he handed me a lumpy manila envelope and a letter. "Tim wanted you to have these." We hugged standing outside beside a picnic table on a pine-needled patch of ground in front of the trailer. The light fell just so, and his shadow lay across the ground just so, that it made me think of the color photograph of his wife and son on the wall above the kitchen table.

"I'll visit again soon," I promised. "Stay warm."

"Go on, now," Jack said. "Don't keep the nuns waiting."

. . .

I rested the side of my head against the cool window of the Greyhound as it hummed down Highway 19 past the familiar landmarks—the last Esso before the end of town, the McHugh fire-watch tower, the low white tanks of the Shell Oil depot receding in row upon row to the east. I remembered that first drive with my parents to Baton Rouge three years ago. It had been this same weather, the same season, the same gray frosted landscape. I remembered, too, before all this happened, how my school bus used to pass the Prejeans's home every day in Zachary, and how I stared out the window hoping for a glimpse of the ailing and mysterious Suzy Prejean. And I remembered sitting in the revolving restaurant at the top of the Riverside Hotel with Chip Benton as we watched the lights of the city drift past outside the dark glass. All these things were in my mind as I opened the envelope on my lap.

Inside were Tim's medals, the ones he'd won in Vietnam.

I turned them over in my fingers. Already they had the look of antiques, like trinkets you might pick up at a yard sale. There was a small brass star attached to a red ribbon, and a round bronze token attached to a yellow ribbon, and another disk attached to a slightly different red ribbon. There were matching rectangular pins for each of these, and a few colorful cloth patches as well. I didn't know what any of it meant. I opened the letter with some trepidation. It was six pages long, written on plain white paper, not the usual airmail kind. "Dear Laura," it began.

Tim said how he sat down to write this letter because he had a bad feeling he might not see me again and he didn't want to leave without saying goodbye and telling me how much I'd meant to him. He'd told his daddy to give me all his medals, because he was afraid if Jack kept them he'd make them out to be something they weren't, like his son was a war hero or something. "I tell you this much, if I die over here you can be sure it was an accident. I'm not taking any chances, not anymore," Tim wrote. He wasn't so foolish that he was going to get himself killed for this army. Because what he'd realized over these past few months was that I was right all along. He'd been sold a line.

"You know I didn't always feel this way, Laura. I started out all gung ho, thinking my country right or wrong, but things kept building until the lies couldn't hold and I'd have to be blind not to see what a genuine fucking disaster this invasion has been." It didn't make any sense, he said. There was nothing there. It was just jungles and hills and villages, and dogs and chickens and people going about their lives. Straw houses and green trees, mothers with babies. "You can't help but think everything would've been fine if we'd just let it be." And yet here they came with their millions of tons of machinery and ordnance, blowing things up indiscriminately and digging themselves in deeper and deeper until they were up to their necks in shit, and as far as Tim could see, it was mostly their own shit. Charlie'll have the last laugh yet, he said: "Lookee crazy American up to neck in own shitee!" But what Tim wanted to know now was, whose idea was this in the first place? Because it was the idea of a madman, that much was clear. He couldn't see any other way to explain it. "This war is the dream of a madman."

I stopped reading and looked out the window. Fields of broken sugarcane blurred past. The bus swayed and hummed. Could there really be a war on, I wondered, right now, with boys like Tim fighting and dying? He was right, it seemed mad. Impossible. I turned to the next page. It was only words on paper, but I could hear his voice as clear as if he were sitting beside me.

"It's raining now," he told me. "The water falls in strings from the edge of the roof outside my door, like one of those bead curtains you see. I'm hoping it keeps raining until the roads are impassable and our next mission gets delayed a day or two. The rain's brought some cool air with it. A rooster's crowing like it's morning and there's a radio playing Bob Dylan in the next hooch. . . .

"I tell you, Laura, if any good comes out of our being here it'll be a complete accident. What I mean is, any good that happens here, happens not because of the U.S. Army but in spite of it. The weird thing is that there *is* some good here. Only it's not what you'd expect. It's got nothing to do with the war. I swear, I believe I spent some of the happiest, most peaceful moments of my life right here in Vietnam. I wonder if you can believe that?

"It's like this," he went on. "You hike out in a field some morning to take a piss. You're half awake, and you can already sense the heat of the day at the back of your neck, but right now it's still cool and a white mist is rising up from the grass all around you so that it's like you're walking in the clouds. And then from out of nowhere a flock of brown baby ducks comes waddling past, tripping over each other and quacking soft. A minute later a mamasan comes up the hill after them wearing a straw hat and a yellow sarong, waving a bamboo stick, quiet as a ghost, humming to herself. She stops on the hill when she sees you. You look at her, and you look at the ducks, and she looks at the ducks, and she looks at you, and she sees you holding your thing in your hand. And then she cracks up and puts her hand over her mouth to stop herself from laughing. And you laugh with her because you're peeing, and the morning is so damn beautiful, and people are so damn great.

"Or it's like Binh, that kid I got to know when we were out on a long mission last year. I told you about him. How he used to come every day and I taught him how to use the radio. Just some local kid from the village, barely spoke any English. I don't think he'd hardly ever been to school, but sharpest mind you ever saw. It's like he had a natural intelligence for working with things. I'd take the radio apart while he was watching and he'd put it back together fast as you please. Wouldn't let me help him. We tried to get him to drink beer but he wouldn't. Most decent kid you ever met. We got to be real good friends, and that didn't have nothing to do with him being Vietnamese or me being American or this damn war that put me here.

"And meeting someone like Binh, you have to assume that there's more like him, and then from that you have to assume that even north of the DMZ they got their Binhs. And then pretty soon you're wondering what makes the enemy so different from me? Probably just like with me, somebody got him all riled up with a bunch of noise, put a gun in his hand and said, Go kill. And you can bet they've got their heroes, their honor, and their medals just like we do. Only what they call bravery we call treachery, and what we call bravery no doubt they call treachery. Only difference is which side of the line you're on. That's something I guarantee Uncle Sam would rather not have you think about.

"Then you get to wondering, Laura, if they can lie to me about that, and do it so damn well and convincing, then what else is a lie? What if everything we've ever been taught as true is a lie? A made-up story? Because we make them up all the time here, believe me.

"The government surely never intended this, but they're schooling some mighty skeptical boys over here, guys who from now on will look sideways at everything you present them with because they've been handed nothing but shit for so long that they won't take nothing for granted anymore. That could actually be the best thing the army has done, taken people like me and turned them into doubters. After two years here, I finally know there's nothing in this world worth dying for except maybe love."

I was shivering as I read, hunched over the pages and sniffling against the cold. The bus rocked as it veered into downtown Baton Rouge. I turned to the last page.

"Laura, you haven't written me for a while. I hardly can blame you, my letters haven't been very cheery lately. And then all I've talked about is how when I get home we're gonna do this and that and I paint this dream of how it's going to be when we're together, but it occurs to me that maybe I should've asked you first before I put you in the middle of that dream. The truth is I don't hardly know you except through your letters. But I guess that's all right. They kept me going. I needed someone to write to, and I always looked forward to getting your reply.

"Course if you're reading this now, hell, none of that hardly makes any difference anymore. But if it helps you to know, I can tell you that if ever I was a little bit kinder or a little bit braver, it was because I had a picture of you in my mind and I wanted to please you. That's what the medals mean. Don't have shit to do with the war.

"So if you ever need any strength in the future, if you ever get to feeling so low you think you aren't worth anything, I hope you take out one of these medals and hold it in your hand and remember that once a boy loved you with all his heart.

"Look in on my dad from time to time if you could. He always liked you.

"I don't want to end this letter—

"Love always,

"Tim."

I stood on the steps in front of the downtown bus station, my suitcase leaning against my leg. This was where I usually caught a taxi to take me to school, but at the moment I couldn't move. I was stunned with loss. It seemed pointless to go forward or back. A door opened behind me and a man in an overcoat passed purposefully down to the sidewalk. The world could go on: I didn't want to. If this was life, I certainly didn't want any more of it. I'd had enough. Like Tim said, what did it matter anyway? You could line us all up—the nun, the soldier, the schoolgirl, the murderer, the good and the bad: we all came to the same end. Why go on? Why even bother if it hurt so much?

Buses rumbled past in front of me, heavy silver tanks with destinations spelled out above their windshields: Lake Charles. New Orleans. I hate to say this, Liz, but I suddenly saw that relief was no more than a few steps away. It would be as easy as taking my next breath. One instant of shock, like jumping into a cold lake, and it'd all be over. Another bus passed trailing black clouds of diesel smoke: Biloxi. What would I miss? Nothing. Who would miss me? Nobody. I would be far, far away, released from all this regret, and whatever was there, even if it was nothing, could only be better than this miserable, ugly life I had now.

I stepped down toward the street and waited for the next bus, shivering in my coat as I readied myself. Could I do it? I believed that I could. The necessary thing, I saw, was to do it all at once and get it right. Another bus was coming, pulling out of the station at the end of the block. I measured the distance from the curb to the middle of the street. Three quick steps was all it would take, like running to the end of a diving board, and then the plunge. And then . . . what? Release. Quiet. Dark. I was conscious of my breath and of the muscles tensing in the back of my legs. I could feel the blood tingling in my fingers at the ends of my hands. Facing me on the opposite side of the road, like a backdrop to this last scene of my life, was a dilapidated row of shops. At the corner stood a barbershop. Next to that, a used bookstore. The last shop in the row was one I must've seen before but never quite registered. "Tattoo" the window said.

It wasn't a matter of choosing, Elizabeth. How do I explain this? It was as if the act had been there all along, in my mind and in my body, only waiting for this moment to be realized. I see it now as one of the few truly inspired moments in my life, a kind of divine intervention that may have literally saved me. Something told me what I had to do, and I did it.

I waited until the bus passed and then hefted up my suitcase and walked directly across the street to the shop. There weren't any lights on but the door was unlocked. A bell tied to the inside doorknob clinked tinnily when I entered.

The front room was dingy and small, with broken linoleum flooring and a few pieces of secondhand furniture. It smelled damp and unclean. Music played from behind a beaded curtain. "Be right there," a voice called. On a low coffee table were scattered some magazines—*Easyriders, Playboy, Rolling Stone*. After a minute a man stepped through the hanging beads, putting on his eyeglasses like he'd just woken up.

He was big and scruffy with pale skin, an unkempt beard, and long reddish hair pulled back in a ponytail. He wore a green army shirt. He looked down at my suitcase. "Yeah?"

"You do tattoos?"

"I do." His voice was lazy, matter of fact, but not coarse.

"Will you give me one?"

He drew his fingers through his beard, like he was combing it. "That depends. Have you got any money?"

"A little."

"What do you want?"

"Can you do words?"

"Sure, I can do words." A flicker of curiosity passed across his eyes when I told him what I wanted. "That's it?"

"Yes."

"Shouldn't be a problem, then. When do you want to do this? Now?"

"Yes. Now."

"Fine. You want to, ah—?" He indicated that I should follow him into the back room. As he held the bead curtain aside, he looked back at my suitcase. "You running away? Not that it's any of my business."

"No."

"Good."

He shooed a cat off an old hospital exam table, draped the table with a towel, and then went to wash his hands in a corner sink. I glanced around the room, my arms folded over my coat, still shivering a little. On the wall were an American flag and a poster of a smiling Buddha. The back of the room was cluttered with junk—a hot plate, an army trunk, some clothes, a standing lamp. Books lay everywhere. On a plywood shelf sat a Panasonic stereo playing a record of jangly folk rock.

"What's your name?"

"Laura."

"I'm Greg. You're eighteen, right?"

"Yes."

He hung up a hand towel and came and turned down the music. "So. How do you want it?"

He explained the colors he had. He showed me an album with tattoo designs on paper, some with lettering. He grabbed a pen and paper and practiced writing out the lines I'd told him. "Something like that?" He had surprisingly good penmanship. "Kind of like, what, Victorian? Edwardian?"

"That's good."

"Hm? Like that? You sure? Okay. Good enough. Where would you like to have this?"

I don't believe I'd ever seen a tattoo on a woman before, and certainly not in the place I had in mind. But like I said, it wasn't a matter of deciding. I knew where it had to go. I ran a finger down below my hip—a spot to mark the night in the parlor when Tim and I had promised ourselves to one another.

"You'll have to, ah, lie back there."

"Take them off?"

"Yeah. Yeah, that'd be better. You might take off your coat, too."

I handed him my coat, and as he hung it up I pulled my blue jeans off and lay back on the cot.

"Little cold in here," he said. "You want a blanket or something?"

"I'm fine."

He turned to a counter to ready his things. I watched from the cot as he drew a long needle from a cloth pouch, looked at it, and chose a different one. He dropped the needle into a steel tray and poured rubbing alcohol over it. Then he turned his attention to the tattoo machine. It was a small, complicated, ugly brass device; it looked like something yanked from a car engine. He hooked the thing up to a black cord that ran to an electric power box on the counter and tested it. It made a harsh buzzing sound, like a dentist's drill. I turned my eyes up to the ceiling, where there was a black-light poster of the stars of the zodiac arrayed around a golden sun against deep blue space. There was Sagittarius, and Scorpio, and Libra . . .

I jerked when something cold touched my skin. "Just gonna clean it with some alcohol," he said. "I'll trace it first with pen and then let you have a look."

He settled himself on a stool by the cot. I could hear his breath sighing in and out of his nose as he drew the words on my skin. "Don't get many girls your age in here," he said. "Don't get many girls at all, actually." He rubbed at my skin with the cotton ball to correct something, and then resumed drawing with the pen. After a minute he sat back. "See what you think." I pushed myself up on my elbows. "I brought the line around down underneath to give it a kind of flourish. . . . I can take that off if you want."

"No. Leave it." I thought it was lovely. Graceful and elegant, like something from a distant, romantic era. I watched as he spread a thin sheen of petroleum jelly over the words. Then he turned back to the counter and squeezed a small amount of red pigment into a tiny tin cup. Last, he removed the needle from the alcohol and fitted it into the machine. I lay back and looked up at the stars.

"You comfortable?" he asked.

"Mm-hm."

He leaned over my hip and brought the tool close to my skin. He buzzed it once or twice and I braced myself for the sting. But then he abruptly stopped and sat back up.

"Look, ah, Laura. You sure about this? It's just, you know, you're not my typical customer." He pushed his glasses up on his nose.

"It's permanent?"

"Permanent."

"Won't ever come off?"

"Not likely."

"Okay then," I said.

"Okay then." He nodded, and I closed my eyes as he lowered the machine and drove the needle home.

"Did it hurt?" you once asked me, Elizabeth.

"Not much," I said.

What I meant, though, and what would've been impossible to explain then, was that it hardly hurt enough. I wanted the hurt. I welcomed the hurt. As the needle scored my skin, I understood for the first time why Saint Catherine of Siena had passed over the crown of gold and seized the one of thorns. There could hardly be pain enough to erase all my misgivings.

The stereo played a slow, waltzlike shuffle. The refrain, I remember, went, "Sad-eyed lady of the lowland," the "low" drawn out in a long, lonely moan that seemed to go on forever. I tried to feel the words as he etched them into me: "I," then "shall," then "but." As he worked, Greg spoke in a soft, even voice, as you might talk to calm a frightened animal.

"People ask for all kinds. Most are pretty predictable, actually. 'Love.' Get that a lot. A heart, a woman's name. Some guys want the name of their unit. 'The Twenty-fifth Infantry Division,' 'Tropic Lightning,' 'Screaming Eagles.' Something like that. 'Semper fi.' That's pretty popular. . . ." He paused to wipe the blood. "Most people, of course, when they think of tattoos they think of sailors. What they don't realize is that tattoos have a long history. Go way back. I've read up on it. The mummies had tattoos. Ancient Egyptians. Greeks. Persians, Polynesians. The Maori. Japanese. American Indians. You name it. You find them in just about any culture, any part of the world, any era. Interesting thing, though, is that different societies have used them to signify different things. As a sign of royalty, for instance. Or spirituality, like for priests, the priestly class. Shamans. They've been used to mark rites of passage. Scarification—you get that a lot in Africa. Same thing as a tattoo, basically. A boy becomes a man. Girls, women. You got tattoos for beauty. Or as charms, magic symbols to bring luck, or prosperity, or love. And then at the totally opposite end of the spectrum, you got your tattoos for outcasts. Criminals. Slaves. Got your Jews, of course . . ."

And then something quite strange happened, something that had never happened to me before and has never happened since. As his voice faded in and out with the music and the buzz of the needle, I felt myself separate from my self. I don't know quite how to explain this. I slipped up out of my body and came to hover somewhere near the ceiling, only the ceiling wasn't there anymore, just an infinitude of space and stars—the universe at my back. Looking down on the table, as if peering through the wrong end of a telescope, I could see a girl. A young woman, in fact. Her dark hair was spread out on either side of her head, her pale winter skin exposed and vulnerable. Her eyes were shut tight, her fists bunched. A red-haired man was bent over her, searing her skin with a needle. I saw that she was trembling, and in that moment my heart went out to her. Brave girl! I wanted to help her, to protect her from harm for the rest of her life. With all the power I could muster, I tried to signal a wish for good to her. *You'll be fine,* I tried to tell her. *Don't worry, you'll be fine. You'll be fine, I promise. I'll take care of you. . . .*

"You're done. It's over," Greg said, and in a flash I was myself again. The needle had stopped buzzing. I could hear the music again, the same song playing the same slow waltz. Below my right hip I felt only a dull burn. "You did real good. That's a sensitive area," Greg said, dabbing carefully at the wound. "You're a real strong lady. Real strong."

At that I finally broke. All the air rushed into me and I sat up with a gasp on the cot as the tears I'd avoided for a week came all at once. I folded over myself, heaving. Greg was taken aback at first. But then, somewhat awkwardly, he cradled his arms around me. He rocked back and forth with me on the cot as I cried, and cried—not out of pain, you understand, or remorse, or even self-pity, but for something more: for the beauty and brevity of life.

Below my hip, still wet with jelly, blood, and ink, was the tattoo you've asked me about so often, but that, until now, I've always put off explaining.

"But what's it mean? Why'd you get it?" you would ask.

"Later. When you're older," I always answered. There seemed too much to say, and to say too little wouldn't do it justice.

Well. Now you are older, Liz, and I hope that with this letter you'll understand at last why it's there and what all it means to me: "I shall but love thee better after death."

XIII

It's getting late, Liz. Your father won't go to bed. I told him I'd wait up, he didn't need to, but he says he's not sleepy. He found an eyeglass repair kit, and now he's repairing all the eyeglasses and sunglasses he can find in the house. It looks like we'll be waiting this out together. He's got the TV on again in the living room, but it's just news about the war, that interminable, mad war.

I have to imagine the best for you, Liz. You're not lugging a suitcase from a bus station to a tattoo parlor. You're not lying unconscious in your black clothes on an empty beach somewhere. You're out having fun with friends, laughing and talking in an all-night diner. Or maybe you're already safe and warm in bed—a friend's bed, or even a lover's. Or maybe you miss your own bed, and even now you're turning the car toward home, coming back to us.

I could stop this letter here—god knows it's long enough. But I'm afraid if I stop now it'll make the story of my adolescence sound like a tragedy, and I don't want to leave you with that impression. There are happier things to tell if I can write a little longer.

Could all our lives be that simple, I wonder? They're only tragedy or comedy depending on where we end them? Here's the rest, Elizabeth, the happy ending.

XIV

The first week back of my last semester at Sacred Heart Academy, during an afternoon PE class, my tattoo became public knowledge.

We'd been running basketball relays in the gym when the tattoo began to bleed. I didn't notice it until we were already in the locker room and I was removing my gym shorts and saw red. The bandage had worked loose, and when it came off, so did the scab, leaving an ugly black scar, like someone had carved up my skin with the point of a steak knife. Blood was dripping down my leg. Obviously this was not your usual menstrual mishap. Girls gasped, the coach was called, and as I was cursing and shouting for paper towels and trying to clean up the mess with my underwear, Sister Agatha stepped into the locker room.

You have to understand, Liz, that in the 1970s normal people like me just didn't get tattoos. Today I know they're almost commonplace; you can hardly go to the shopping mall without seeing dozens of teenage boys and girls flaunting them. Even celebrities wear tattoos nowadays, giving them an air of glamour. But back then, tattoos were reserved for people of only the lowest, most disreputable classes, like prisoners, or prostitutes, or sideshow freaks. They signaled thuggery and vice. So for a girl at a Catholic school to have one was . . . well, it was unheard of. It was outrageous.

For the second time during my stay at SHA, I was dragged by Hagatha-Agatha to the nurse's station. The principal was called. My parents were called. Sister Evelyn couldn't bring herself to use the word *tattoo* over the phone. "It's . . . something . . . your daughter did . . . horrible . . ." she stammered. "You should come immediately."

Nurse Palmer was furious. "I can't understand it. Why you, a young woman, would knowingly inflict this kind of damage to your skin, your own skin! Not to mention the health risks involved . . ." She painted the wound with Mercurochrome and rebandaged it. "Were you drunk?" she asked, and then gave me a tetanus shot, jabbing me with the needle much harder, I thought, than was necessary.

When my parents arrived from Zachary the bandage had to be removed again so they could see. Nuns bent around taking turns to look and recoil in horror. My parents were shocked, of course, but more than that, they were ashamed. They stood as far back from me as the small room allowed, as if they were already taking steps to disown me. When we all moved from the nurse's station to the principal's office, they walked well ahead of me, my mother with her arms folded grimly over her coat, my father close by her side, touching her elbow. "Back to class! Back to class!" Sister Evelyn shouted at the girls who had gathered in the front hall. They gawked as I passed, the girl with the tattoo. I heard my name repeated, passed down from the upperclassmen to the newer girls: "Jenkins . . . Zachary . . . trouble."

I sat on a chair outside the principal's office while my

parents conferred inside with Sisters Evelyn and Agatha. Two Beta Club girls stared at me, entranced, as they slowly sorted mail into teachers' pigeonholes. When Sister Mary Margaret arrived, she shooed them away.

"Laura—" she said, stopping in front of me. The oversized wooden cross swayed against her tunic as she took a moment to collect herself. "First of all, is this true?" I nodded. "And what's written there, is that . . . Browning?"

"He died," I explained. "In Vietnam. Three weeks ago, just before he was supposed to come home."

She brought a hand to her mouth. "Oh dear. Oh dear, you poor child. I'm so sorry."

"There was a funeral, in Zachary. And I didn't . . . You know I didn't plan to do this, Sister."

"No . . ."

"It was something . . . I had to do. For him. It's for him."

She nodded slowly, as if forcing herself to understand. "Yes."

"I didn't have a choice. This is what I had to do. To remind me . . . so I never forget . . . how much he loved me." I looked away. It seemed hopeless. "They won't understand."

Sister Mary Margaret was quiet, as if thinking things through. After a moment she sighed and said, as much to herself as to me, "No. No, I don't suppose they will." I saw her glance anxiously at Sister Evelyn's office. Then she bent down and gave me a hug. "Are you all right here?"

"I'm okay."

"I'll see what I can do," she said and, straightening her back, went in to join the others.

Sister Mary Margaret tried her best for me that day, I'm sure, but it was an impossible defense. She argued that, technically, I had done nothing wrong; there was no prohibition against tattoos in the school handbook. "There's no rule against murderers, either, but we don't allow them in the school," answered Sister Agatha. Sacred Heart Academy, she reminded everyone, didn't even allow girls to wear earrings to school.

Trying to deflect some of the blame onto herself, Sister M&M then confessed her role in the affair. She told how she was the one who had secretly passed letters from the boy in Vietnam, willfully violating the principal's own orders, and thus leading the poor girl down the confused path that brought her to this desperate, grief-stricken end. . . .

The good nun, I found out later, would pay for this admission. But for now, she succeeded only in delaying my immediate expulsion from the school. I was put on disciplinary probation until the academic staff council could meet and decide my fate. That very afternoon, I was sent home with my parents to Zachary, "so as not to disturb the other girls."

It wasn't a happy return home, as you can imagine. I kept to my bedroom, rereading Tim's letters. My parents again wondered where they had gone wrong. At dinner, passing the potatoes and string beans, they tried not to look directly at me, the tattooed lady sitting at their table. Sister M&M phoned occasionally regarding the status of my case; the academic staff council wouldn't meet until Friday afternoon, but in the meantime she was trying to lobby the other teachers on my behalf. It didn't look promising. I had been suspended once before. And as a work-study student, admitted only through the charity of the nuns, I was already practically provisional. It wasn't like I was the daughter of an important alumna, a legacy student; SHA could let me go without much fuss.

For myself, the tragedy wasn't so much in the prospect of losing my diploma from SHA as it was in losing my chance to enter LSU. I had been awarded a small scholarship in the Journalism Department, and being expelled from high school would certainly mean forfeiting that. The university might not even accept me at all after this. I saw myself becoming the tattooed outcast everyone already thought I was, slinking around dark alleyways, thin and mean and full of sin.

You remember the charity cases, Liz. I can't credit myself for the actions they took. When I first arrived at SHA, I had clung to them only as castaways in a life raft must cling to one another. It was instinctual, necessary—not born of any special generosity or sacrifice on my part. That's why what they did for me seemed that much more surprising and, in retrospect, that much more valorous.

The first was Soo Chee Chong. She slipped away from campus after her last class one day midweek and found her way downtown. It must have been far more difficult for her to enter the shop than it had been for me. I had no choice; Soo Chee did. I can imagine what she must have been feeling, considering all that was at stake: her parents' reputations, their standing in the local Chinese community, her own position as the first of her family to be educated in America. She would've had plenty of doubts waiting in that dingy front room, seeing the biker and girlie magazines on the coffee table. Meeting Greg, she thrust the piece of notebook paper into his hand. Greg was cautious—he made sure she knew what she was doing. "Yes. Of course, I know. Let's begin," Soo Chee said, hopping up onto the cot. The poster of the Buddha put her strangely at ease as Greg talked her through the painful procedure. When she arrived at school the following day, she proudly showed everyone what she'd done: there, high on her left breast, was her name spelled out in Chinese characters—Soo Chee Chong, the beautiful sound of jade.

Anne Harding, who'd had her brace removed that year, and who was rumored to be a candidate for class valedictorian, was the second to go. Was it easier for her, after Soo Chee had gone first? I doubt it. I see her marching through the front door of the tattoo parlor, stoic and brave, to put her request to Greg. "Mark me here," she might've said, jabbing her finger low at the back of her neck where her skin had been covered up for three years by the padding of her brace. In an elegant Parisian art deco script entwined with green vines and small red buds, hers read, "It made me stronger."

The next was Christy Lee. She skipped morning classes the following day, and when she returned to campus after lunch she was wearing a permanent chain around her upper left arm. That was all, no lettering. At the outside of her arm, where you could easily see it, the chain was broken and the two ends dangled free.

The nuns tried to send the girls home, but they refused to go, and instead brought three chairs from the library, placed them deliberately on the front lawn of the school near one of the oak trees, and sat. The girls' parents were summoned, and there were threats and tears and raised voices. Still, the girls wouldn't budge. Soo Chee's mother, a small, elegantly dressed woman, tried to drag Soo Chee from her chair, tilting it sideways onto two legs, but Christy

Lee grabbed hold of Soo and wouldn't let go. The parents retreated to the principal's office to try and figure out what to do next. The girls, settling in, took out their books and notebooks and began studying for an upcoming trigonometry test and drafting letters to the editors of the local school newspapers.

When a Cathedral High School photographer, the one who'd taken Chip's place, came by at noon to take pictures, Sister Evelyn tried to block his entry to campus. But he put up a fight, shouting about the freedom of the press, until the classes at the front of the building were disrupted; the principal decided it would be less trouble to let him take his photos. Attracted by the disturbance, other girls wandered out between bells to chat with those on the lawn; some brought their lunches with them, sat, and stayed. In the afternoon, boys driving home from CHS slowed their cars on the road in front to see what was going on. They honked their horns and shouted from their windows at the girls milling on the lawn; the girls shouted and waved back.

You couldn't call it a protest exactly, Anne Harding said, keeping me posted by phone. But clearly the nuns were getting nervous. Sister Evelyn seemed to be trying to wait them out, hoping the trouble would blow over if she just ignored them. But instead of blowing over, it grew.

Before the week's end, four more girls made their way downtown. A frizzy-haired girl named Lisa, who idolized Janis Joplin, got a rose on her right ankle. Another got a small, discreet dove on her hip. The third girl got a cross with a crown of thorns, dripping blood, on her shoulder blade. When they arrived at campus, wearing their bandaged tattoos like badges of honor, these girls didn't even bother going to their homeroom classes, but went straight to the front lawn to join the charity cases, who'd since equipped themselves with blankets and thermoses of cocoa. Most surprising of all was when Traci Broussard, cheerleader and CHS-SHA homecoming queen, who we'd always considered the luckiest and most enviable girl in our class, arrived Friday morning with her own tattoo, a heart broken in two under a banner that said *"Les blessures d'amour durent pour toujours"*—love's wounds last forever. She solemnly took her place in the circle with the charity cases, sitting knee-to-knee with them in her stadium coat, and quietly wept for much of the day, no one knew why.

Christy Lee declared it a sit-in and said they wouldn't return to classes until the academic staff council allowed me back at school. Someone strung up a bed sheet in the oak tree, "Justice for Laura Jenkins!" Word spread, and more girls abandoned their books and pencils and streamed out onto the lawn, effectively canceling classes for the rest of the day. Anxious mothers of freshmen arrived by car to take their daughters home; they'd seen such things on TV and they never ended well. Boys from CHS began trickling over, and by Friday afternoon the crowd had grown to several dozen. A couple of boys with especially long hair strummed guitars and sang protest songs as they imagined the hippies did. They got up chants, girls made speeches, and the senior class president wrote a poem to commemorate the occasion, called "The Winter of Our Discontent." Anne Harding told me that Sister Mary Margaret had been spotted at the window of her second-story classroom, watching the goings-on with a faint but unmistakable smile on her face. It was a wholly peaceful demonstration, marred only when a boy named Randy, who people said was high on marijuana, fell from a tree and broke his wrist. The sixties had come at last to Sacred Heart Academy.

My only regret is that I wasn't there to see it, stuck as I was at home in Zachary. But "it was huge," Anne assured me. A Channel 9 reporter came with a cameraman to cover the story, and it made the evening news that night, prompting my parents to cluck their tongues in disapproval. No wonder, they said, that I'd gone bad, considering the school I was in. What were those nuns thinking, letting the girls run wild like that? It only proved, my father said, what he suspected all along, that the pope was aligned with the Jews and hippies to hand the country over to the Communists.

But the sit-in worked. At their meeting Friday afternoon, the academic staff council found itself in a quandary. As much as they disapproved of the girls' actions, the school couldn't very well expel all the students who had tattoos now. Traci Broussard? Anne Harding? Soo Chee Chong? Impossible. So they voted to rescind my probation; I would be allowed to return to school on Monday morning and could graduate with my class after all. But they ordered that the school handbook be revised immediately to make explicit the policy regarding tattoos, clearly stating that, in line with its Catholic mission to provide a sound academic and moral education for young ladies, the school would henceforth bar any girl with a tattoo, visible or not, from attending Sacred Heart Academy.

"We won!" Christy Lee said over the phone that night. "Power to the people!" Sacred Heart would never be the same, she insisted. The administration could never again take the students for granted; they weren't anybody's slaves; from now on, their voices would have to be heard. In fact, Christy had already spoken to some of the other girls about starting a black student caucus at the campus. "It's about time, don't you think?" she asked.

. . .

Well. It wasn't over yet. As you must know by now, Liz, such an upset to the accepted order of things can't go unanswered. The next week there were angry visits and calls to the principal's office, and letters to the editor of the local *Morning Advocate* deploring the shocking "tattoo incident" at one of the city's most venerable institutes of secondary education. Psychologists weighed in with theories of sadomasochism and mass hysteria. The alumnae association got involved, the PTA got involved. A couple of fathers of students were prominent local attorneys, and they got involved. Three of the girls who'd gotten tattoos, it turned out, were under eighteen. The consensus among the parents and school administration was that someone, somewhere, had to pay. And as you must know, too, Liz, it's easy enough to find a scapegoat. Just look for the person with the lowest standing, someone a bit scruffy who lives at the edge of society. In Hester Prynne's day they might have locked the culprit up in the stockade, or tarred and feathered him and run him out of town on a rail. We, though, being an advanced civilization, have a thing called the criminal justice system. Within a week, Greg Renfroe, big gentle Greg, was arrested and his tattoo parlor shut down. He was quickly brought to trial and sentenced to nine months in the parish jail on trumped-up charges of corruption of minors and moral turpitude.

And Sister Mary Margaret, the kindest, most compassionate nun at Sacred Heart, and the only one who, as far as I was concerned, was really worthy of her habit—what became of her? At the end of the school year, Sister M&M was quietly transferred to an elementary school in El Paso, Texas, on the Mexican border. In a letter to me that summer, she sounded amazingly sanguine about the whole affair. She was looking forward to meeting her new students, she wrote. From what she'd seen so far, any skills she had as an English teacher would be especially useful there. She counseled me to stick to the Romantics; they'd never let me down, no matter what anyone else said. She closed, "Be good, and if you can't be good, at least be sensible."

XV

Well. That's about it, the essentials anyway. It hasn't always been a pleasant story, I know. I suppose that's one reason I haven't told any of this to you until now. And I'm afraid it's fallen short of my promise to give you the "truth about life." At best, I've only given you the truth, or at least part of the truth, of one life. But maybe that's the closest any of us can get to knowing the big Truth.

It's approaching midnight. Your father has made chamomile tea for us. He came in and rubbed my shoulders for a minute. He sits watching from the sofa now, sipping his tea, wondering when I'll put down the pen. He looks at me curiously. Soon, soon.

My tattoo, thirty years old, has faded with age, but sometimes I swear I can still feel it throbbing, like it wants to tell me something. I seem to feel it now telegraphing a message as I sit by this window waiting for you to come home—a reminder, maybe, or a warning: "I shall but love thee better . . . I shall but love thee better . . ."

I ran into Greg again after that, by the way. It was in the admissions office at LSU, where I went to work while I studied for my BA. He had enrolled in the school of social work, and would drop by from time to time to say hello. He was hired as a counselor at Louisiana Training Institute, the place where they send juvenile delinquents. He's still there, as far as I know.

And even today I'll meet a charity case now and then. Soo Chee, Anne Harding, Christy Lee: we all turned out all right, every one of us. We pass each other at the mall, or pushing our shopping carts down the aisle of the supermarket. We nod and smile at one other like we're sharing a secret. *Look at us,* the smile says. *We survived. The scarred ones. The lucky ones.*

Because it's true, Liz. We've been so lucky until now. So lucky. I keep thinking of those poor women on TV, crying and shaking their fists in the air. It's not for themselves they cry, you know. Mothers don't care about their own pain, but for the pain of the son who was tortured, or the husband who was shot. The pain of the daughter who's run away.

You never tell me, Liz, but I know. You're fifteen, you're a girl, so you hurt. It's the fate of all girls, and it's what in the end makes us women. Small consolation to you now, perhaps, but what else can a mother say? Things will be better. Things will be better. Don't worry, you'll be fine, I promise.

Well. I'll finish this letter now. I intend to leave the pages on your bed so you can find them when you come home. Maybe you'd prefer a new cellphone for your birthday, but this is what you'll get. Know, though, that all this doesn't begin to say how much I love you.

It's never too late to change, Liz. We could begin now by simply deciding to talk to one another. That's all, just talk. It'd be as easy as taking a breath. As easy as turning the page.

I hear a car approaching. Your father sits up on the

couch. Is it you? It could be you. I imagine your return. Lights sweep through the living room as you turn up the drive, and we rush out to meet you. Tears, hugs, forgiveness.

Welcome home, daughter.

Love always,
Mom

ABOUT THE AUTHOR

GEORGE BISHOP holds an MFA from the University of North Carolina at Wilmington, where he won the department's Award of Excellence for a collection of stories. He has spent most of the past decade living and teaching overseas in Slovakia, Turkey, Indonesia, Azerbaijan, India, and Japan. He now lives in New Orleans.